Chains that Bind

Written by Amy Jones

Edited by Kamille John & Grace Jones

Illustrated by Kenny Durant

Graphic Design by Jonathan Greenidge

Dedication

This book is dedicated to Caribbean readers all around the world, who have always been intrigued by our folklores of *jumbies* and the like.

CONTENTS

Acknowledgements

Not to sound cliché, but I acknowledge Yahweh's blessings on me, with this ability He has given me. Acknowledgements are also due to Kamille, for her review and constructive criticism during this publication process.

Furthermore, let me also acknowledge and express my gratitude to my dear Kenny, whose unending support and belief in me, makes seemingly impossible things possible.

Prologue

"James?" Janice called for a second time, "James, you dey?"

"Yeah, ah dey." James finally responded.

"How you get quiet so, baby?" Janice questioned. The concern could be heard in her voice over the phone.

"Ah jus' tired, girl." James lied.

"You sure?" She asked, even more concerned. "You know if somet'ing happen, or if somet'ing bot'erin' you, you could tell me, eh?"

"Yes, baby. Ah know. You doh ha' to worry." James knew he was wrong for keeping this from his wife, but somehow, he felt like he had to. Every time he tried to be honest, it was like a thread was pulled to sew his lips shut. James knew something was wrong, but the more he tried, the worst he felt.

"Well if everyt'ing okay, ah goin' an' put dem girls to sleep." Janice responded, "Is minutes to eight, an' you know how Cherry *head hard* ahready. Ah love you, you hear?"

"Ah love you too, baby. Kiss dem for me eh."

"Yes, ah go do dat. How long again?" Janice asked, as she did since her husband left. She knew the duration he was scheduled to be in San Souci, but somehow, hearing his words reassured her that he would return, and return soon.

"Janice, only ah week ah go, you know. Tomorrow – Saturday, makin' it two weeks." James responded, but Janice sighed. It was a deep, melancholic sigh that broke his heart as it did every time.

He took the opportunity to make her feel secured in the fact that one way or the other, he would see her soon.

"Six months go go by fas' ah tell you. Doh worry. We go see soon."

Suddenly, James felt a cold shiver over his shoulder, travelling down to his spine and into his legs. He knew that feeling.

"Janice, ah ha' to go."

Click. Before she could respond, the phone was disconnected.

James sighed, he turned around to see the long flowing white dress hoovering over his window. It was happening again, and he couldn't help the pull he felt towards *her*. As she hoovered away, he trembled. Fear gripped him in a way nothing else had ever done.

He wanted to tell Janice how he felt and what he was experiencing but it was almost as if he couldn't. No matter how hard he tried, the words could never come out clearly. And then he thought about her temper and that she would think he was just making the perfect excuse for having another woman.

He thought to himself that even if Janice suggested such a thing, she would be wrong because she knew James loved her more than he loved anyone else. Maybe if it was up for debate and discussion, he had loved his children equally or maybe a little more than he had loved her, but there was no one else. He would never do a thing to *intentionally* jeopardize their relationship.

As his thoughts raced and his fears gradually subsided, James drifted off to sleep. At 3 a.m., James was awoken to the feeling of the strange presence in his room. It was the similar feeling he had earlier while on the phone with his wife. He rose off the bed – eyes bright and blazing; he was in a trance, *again*.

He walked towards the window, crawled through the opened space and planted his feet on the wet grass. It was cold, but he didn't feel it. His eyes were glued on the beautiful young woman, adorned in the long, white dress. It was night but the young woman's head sported a big straw hat that covered the majority of her face.

He walked towards the bushes right ahead of the San Souci Great River and was lost behind the trees that overlooked the flowing water. As the woman stripped her clothes and entered the cold water, James did the same.

And as it happened, in times past, at the break of dawn, James would wake up at the mouth of the river, lost and confused. He would have to search for his clothes and make his way back to the house. He felt embarrassed, confused and violated. What had happened? Why couldn't he remember? And worse yet, why wasn't *papa God* listening to his prayers to stop this woman from taking advantage of him?

He had planned that morning to leave the island as his last working day was the day before. One way or the other, he was getting out of that place and never returning.

AMY J.W. JONES

1 Home Sweet Home

Sunday morning was a cold morning on the beautiful, tiny 70-square-mile island of Grenada. The tall coconut trees under the mountainous terrains swayed in the morning breeze against a blue-sky background. A chilly breeze blew through the small community of BrownsVille that was situated on the north eastern end of the island.

BrownsVille was adorned by many trees: cocoa trees, five-finger trees, golden-apple trees, mango trees, French cashew trees, water-nut trees and Grenada's black gold – nutmeg. The picturesque island from the view of the small community, looked like something straight out of a travel destination magazine. It was something about that place that made the tourists love the island even more.

Again, the cold breeze rushed through the small house that belonged to Janice Hopkins, and she shivered. Indeed, the February breeze was out of the ordinary. It was so cold, Janice began making jokes that snow would soon fall on the island. It was the first time in many years in BrownsVille that villagers were shivering and walking around with extra clothing.

It was 7:15 a.m. and the tall, slender Petra Hopkins was just coming out of her room. Short, plump Cherry Hopkins and the muscular James Jr. Hopkins both crawled out of their rooms, then greeted each other as they journeyed to the kitchen to fill their aching stomachs. That morning, there was no fruit juice in the juice mug on the table, but a pot of boiling *cocoa tea* on the stove which Janice made to keep the children warm. It was much needed!

No matter how old they were, cocoa tea always seemed to make the day of Grenadian children. Twenty-one-year-old Petra sat on the chair next to James Jr., or JJ as they called him, who was still dozing off with *cacajay* in his eyes.

"Boy wake up dey!" Petra shouted, "When time for you to sleep in de nite, you dey on computer talkin' to people. Get up dey! An' go and wash out da cacajay in you' eye an' dat *bavay* around you mout' too eh."

JJ mumbled insults under his breath but did as he was told. He was eight years old, and very mature for his age. In two months he was going to turn nine but if one saw him, one would think he must have been twelve. No matter how much he disliked her discipline, JJ respected his sister Petra, because she was the second in command at home to his mother, Janice.

JJ never knew his father; in fact, of the four who lived in the house, JJ was the only one who did not meet his father, James. His older sister Cherry was seven years old when their father left, but there were few things she remembered about him. Petra frequently said that she couldn't seem to remember anything much about him except for his eyes and the smell of his cologne. But everyone knew she lied.

Petra was thirteen years old when James left for San Souci and never returned. It was her hurt and her disappointment in him that caused her to constantly pretend like she didn't remember him. To her, thinking about him less meant that she would eventually forget him, but that never seemed to work.

Everyone in the community of BrownsVille on the island of Grenada had an opinion on what really transpired. There was talk that he was dead. Some said he ran off from his family and used the job as an excuse. Ms. Jennifer, the neighbourhood seamstress, even said that he must have been secretly gay and went to meet his lover in San Souci.

Some said he was fed up of his family, knowing how short Janice's temper was, while others, like the neighbourhood gossip, Ms. Millie, suspected that James ran off with another woman. But according to Janice, James had gone to the neighbouring island of San Souci for a job he was offered. As far as she knew, he said he would return in six months but that six months turned into eight years and everything changed.

Indeed, it had been eight years since James left Grenada and Janice never spoke about him, while Petra pretended like he didn't exist. It was hard for Cherry and JJ to feed their curiosity as they didn't know much about him either. It mattered not how much they begged, Petra would never share. The truth was sometimes Petra grew sadder and sadder when she talked about her father and she longed to safeguard her younger siblings from getting attached to the idea of him as she once did.

Occasionally, Janice would make jokes about Petra *stickin' up in she fadda skin like ah tick*. But the stories shared were always vague, so when the children didn't get the information they needed from their elder sister and mother, there was always Miss Millie.

Miss Millie was the closest neighbour to the Hopkins and she was quite an inquisitive one at that! Miss Millie was a nice lady on most days but she and Janice *couldn't pull* anymore. Before the distance between them became evident, Miss Millie and Janice were good friends. They weren't *ridin' buddies*, but they used to watch out for each other.

That stopped happening when Miss Millie started spreading rumours in the small community of BrownsVille about Janice. Miss Millie spoke to her cousin Florence about James, Florence told Janice's cousin Greta, who eventually (like ol' people on the island of Grenada say), *brought back news* for Janice.

On one occasion, Cherry came from school very sad about the trouble she got into with her teacher, Miss Farray. She walked up the dirt path to her home with her head hanging low; Miss Millie saw her, immediately looked out the window and shouted,
"Chil' wa do you? Wa you hangin' you head low in shame so for? And watch how you stretchin' you lip lang lang as Pearl's air strip! Chil', the last time ah see somebody do dat was when ah see Janice doin' dat when you fadda leave her."

Janice and James had been married for eighteen years, ten of which they spent together. And although she missed him, she never expressed her feelings for her children, and especially Miss Millie, to see. The children found it interesting to hear stories from Miss Millie but Janice had warned them about her. She often said it had nothing to do with their beef, but the fact that Miss Millie seldom had good things to say about anyone.

On top of that, Cherry and JJ never liked getting in grown folks' business, so they always tried their best not to ask Janice much about her and their father's business. The few times Cherry asked her, she embarrassed her so much Cherry tried her best not to do it again.

Occasionally, Miss Millie would say things about James around the children with the expectation that they would trade information about Janice. *That wicked woman.* When Cherry was younger, she always fell victim to the tricks of Miss Millie but the older she got, the wiser she became when it came to her. Just a few weeks prior, Miss Millie waited until JJ passed her yard to say to him,

"But JJ, just as you and you fadda ha' de same name, is just so you and he look alike you know. Same walk, same talk, same behaviour, same how you fadda used to put he hand over he head when he used to be sleepin' in the hammock in the veranda, just so you used to do the same thing too when ah used to babysit you. But ah hope you doh come out like him and walk out on you family. Ah realize you *ha' real wayward ways.*"

Leave it to Miss Millie to think that she was smart, but little did she know that the children were always one step ahead of her. JJ just looked at her, told her good afternoon, and kept on walking.

~

A rush of cold breeze came through the kitchen window, blowing the peach kitchen curtain into the air and removing the tissue off the plate that was covering the coconut bakes. The smell filled the nostrils of everyone, making their mouths salivate. Cherry could feel the saliva gushing down her throat the same way the *water nut* used to gush down her throat when she, Petra and JJ drank them.

She was *very* hungry, so she reached over the table to take her slice, when she felt **pax!!!** It was one hot slap across her hand; it stung. It felt just the way her arm felt last month when the *mybones* stung her while she was climbing the five-finger tree.

"Like you start to lose you respect eh little girl?" Janice asked, and she was not expecting an answer. "Ent we does pray before we eat here? Watch girl! *Doh play de beast wid de long ears eh!*"

Cherry pulled her hand back quickly and began rubbing it, but the embarrassment stung more than the slap. Janice had a way of looking at her children when she said the simplest of things and making them feel like they were on trial for murder. As for Cherry and Janice, they did not have a good relationship. Janice stayed out of Cherry's way and Cherry always made sure that she did as she was told.

Despite their differences, Cherry didn't joke around when Janice mentioned *prayers*; she was a praying woman so the moment she made mention of anything that had to do with the spiritual realm, all jokes had to cease.

"Sorry." Cherry replied as she hung her head in shame.
"Since she so *hungry mouth*, let she pray." Petra lashed back at Cherry.
Cherry didn't even bother to argue with Petra. It was just as that inquisitive neighbour, Miss Millie used to say, *"as similar as JJ is to he fadda, just so Petra dey like she mudda."*

According to Miss Millie, Janice could have easily had Petra on her own and James have JJ on his own. Cherry, according to Miss Millie, took an equal amount of everything from both parents.

With all the things one would hear Miss Millie saying about the Hopkins, it could be easily assumed that Miss Millie wouldn't have a care when it came to Janice. One could think that someone on the island like Miss Millie would *bad talk* her enemy when they disagreed, but not Miss Millie.

According to her, the respect she had for Janice would not allow her to be bothered by their simple misunderstanding. Yet, for others, this only created the assumption that there was something Janice had against Miss Millie, or there was something Miss Millie was hiding.

It did not take JJ long before he too became inquisitive and forgot Janice's constant reminder: *Take you nose out people business if it en ha' no place dey.* But JJ and Miss Millie's son Marcus were good friends, so one day, he asked Marcus why he believed their mothers did not talk.

Not too long after, Marcus came back to say to JJ, "me mother say to tell you that your mother too selfish."
JJ laughed and turned to Marcus, "Da is a lie boy. Me mother say you mother too fass and that is somet'ing none of us could deny!"

"Hurry up and pray na girl!" JJ shouted from across the table as Cherry bolted out of her day dream.
"For these and all other gifts to us, God's holy name we praise, amen."

~

It was a quarter to nine when Janice and her children arrived at the Triscalone House of Prayer. The church was located on Pierre Drive, a few minutes away from the Hopkins' residence. If it was one thing about Mrs. Janice Hopkins, it was her time management. She was always early for whatever she had to do and wherever she was going. Her cousin Susan always said that Janice was the first woman she ever knew to be early to her own wedding.

Janice walked towards the entrance of the church and looked around before entering the building. She was looking for Sister Mary, or Aunty Mae as the children called her.

"Morning Aunty Mae!" Cherry shouted as she saw the short dark-skinned old woman wobbling towards them.

"Morning love." Mary responded. "How allu do?"

"Go in allu class." Janice interjected as she shooed the trio so she could talk to Mary.

"How you doin' today, Janice?"

"Not too bad." Janice lied.

In fact, she hadn't slept all week. She had been tossing and turning for some strange reason. She felt unsettled in her spirit and she needed to talk to Mary, who had become like a mother to her.

"Talk to me before church start." Mary insisted.

"Ah doh know what it is but de more ah t'ink as de days go by ah go feel better, the worse ah feel." Janice started. "Ah feelin' alone an' ah feelin' hurt an' sometimes ah cyah help but take it out on de chil'ren."

Tears streamed down Janice's face and Mary took her to the back of the church and into the prayer room.

"Come me chil'" she said, "come let we pray. Prayer does do ah lot, an' you know it."

As the children walked through the door, the warmth of the church could be felt, not physically, but emotionally. The warmness of the hearts of the people felt genuine. Everyone smiled and said good morning, inquiring how the week had been and what plans were ahead, each with the encouragement of *"God bless you."* The friendliness of the people was infectious and since the Hopkins began going to church there, they never left. The family used to attend the Greystone Evangelistic Deliverance Temple but whenever they did, JJ and Cherry preferred to stay home.

When Cherry was younger, she used to pretend to be sick so she could stay home. Talk about unfriendly *church people!* The family went to GED Temple for two years and to this day, there were still people who would pass them in the streets like they were non-existent. Ironically enough, those same people had the audacity to pride themselves as the friendliest and most welcoming church. *Eh fwere!* What was interesting and captivating about Triscalone House of Prayer, other than the love the family received, was the interactive and down-to-earth delivery of Pastor Samuels; his wisdom always compelled the congregation to listen.

~

At ten minutes to twelve, Janice and her children walked down the dirt path in Brownsville to their home. The village was beautiful. Of all the places in Grenada, it had a special sense of soul. The Hopkins lived on Conch street, and apart from the little issue with Janice and Miss Millie, everybody genuinely loved each other. The villagers knew the Hopkins children from the time they were born. None of the people on the street had changed.

There was Mr. John and Mrs. Agatha Donald whose daughter Lucinda was studying medicine in Cuba. They always boasted about her achievements whenever they met up with the villagers.

Mrs. Donald used to say, "Cherry girl, study you head. *Study you head to lif' you mudda nose* like how Donna lif'in' ours."

Lower down to the Donalds were Samantha and her two children, Paul and Phoebe. No one could quite understand how Samantha did it - she worked, studied and managed to make time for her children. Samantha always spoke about her missed opportunities and how foolish she was to let her children's father convince her that her education was not of paramount importance. It did not take Sammy long to realise that he didn't want a woman who was more educated than him. He wanted her to stay at home so he could *fe-o-lay*. He persuaded her to have children, putting a halt on her Associate's Degree in Public Health.

Millanie Jacobs, who everyone called Miss Millie, lived adjacent Sammy with her son Marcus. Her house directly faced the Hopkin's residence. Every so often, Miss Millie's common law husband Winston would pass by and then he would be gone again. But no one knew much about him, and that was the thing about Miss Millie: she tried to know everything about everybody but kept everything about herself from everyone.

Right at the back of the Hopkins' house lived Joel McIntosh, the oldest man in the village. Everyone referred to him as Mr. Joe and the younger ones called him Ol' Man Joe. To others, the nickname may have sounded like an insult, but Mr. Joe didn't mind. The Hopkins children had a special love for Mr. Joe; he had been around all their lives. He didn't speak as often but he always knew a way to make them laugh. Sometimes when he was making his early trip to look after his bull, he could be heard whistling the same tune:

> *Come leh we go; fish in de sea for so!*
> *Come leh we go; cock in tree ah crow!*

He was like an alarm; sometimes JJ thought Mr. Joe used to purposefully do it. Whenever Mr. Joe started his whistling JJ would suck his teeth and pull his pillow over his head. Mr. Joe would laugh and when the whistling wasn't loud enough, he would come by the back step and say,

"Morning Janice. Morning chil'ren."

"Morning Mr. Joe." They would say.

"Fore-day morning go ahready. It doh good to make de sun get up before you."

Mr. Joe had a theory that the people who got up after 6am were lazier than those that got up before the sun rose. Petra never believed him until one morning she took Mr. Joe's advice and got up at 6am. She said her prayers, washed her face and took out Laura the sheep. She helped her mother cook and then, she went to work. That was the most productive day she said she had in a while. Ever since then, she tried her best to get up as early as she could to start her day. She tried to teach JJ and Cherry that Mr. Joe was right, but they were too lazy to comply.

~

As Janice walked ahead on their way home, JJ, Petra and Cherry were dragging their feet along not too far behind her. JJ and Cherry talked about the new games they played in Sunday school with Teacher Mindy, and Petra spoke about the project the junior adults had to do on *Relationship Rules*.

Without warning, Janice suddenly stopped dead in her tracks, as if she had seen something that startled her. The children were a little way off from the house but could see that

Janice's eyes were glued to their small concrete structure. *What on earth was she looking at?* It was almost as if Janice had seen a ghost. JJ looked at Cherry and Cherry looked at Petra; they then hurried to their mother with great concern.

"Mammy, wa do you?" Cherry asked. When she did not respond, Cherry turned to her siblings, "Allu wa do mammy?"

They focused their eyes in the same direction Janice's eyes wandered and it immediately fell on the tall figure standing in the veranda. Whomever or whatever it was seemed to startle Petra too.

"JJ, who dey?" Cherry questioned her brother.

JJ turned to Cherry with a look on his face, as if to say, *"wa do da chupid gyal?"* then responded, "Cherry how ah go kno?". Me and you was all in de back! Ah doh know who dey but ah goin' and see."

JJ was cautious but fearless, while Cherry was timid and coward. She never liked confrontations and was scared of almost everything. She was scared of insects, needles, snakes, kittens, exams, *licks,* homework. Man, if you could name it, Cherry probably had a reason to be afraid of it. She was even more scared of the silhouette they saw standing in their veranda. JJ walked up to the house and Cherry trailed behind him; and for a big sister, it was shameful that her little brother was the protector.

"Wey all goin'?" Janice finally spoke. "Come back here!"

But by the time she could stop them, JJ was already on the step inquiring from the person who he was and what he wanted. Janice walked forward towards the house holding Petra by the hand. Cherry looked back to see Petra wincing in pain as Janice gripped her hand firmly. She turned around and walked closer and closer to the house, the shadowy figure seemed to take form. It was a man.

From the distance, he did not look like anyone they knew from the village. He walked towards JJ and Cherry moved forward. Janice was just a few steps away with Petra. Cherry's eyes fixed on the man who was staring at JJ. He took his khaki cap off his head and put down the Adidas bag he was carrying. Tears streamed down Cherry's face when she realised who the man was.

"Daddy?" Cherry was startled.

It was almost as if she was looking at JJ forty years ahead. She looked at JJ and he looked back at Cherry with a look of confusion. She didn't need anyone to tell her who he was. She didn't need Janice or Petra to tell her that she was looking at her father because she knew for herself that it was him. Just as Miss Millie said, JJ looked just like him and he looked just like JJ.

"Aye Cherry-oh." The man responded.

She had not heard that in years and it seemed like all the memories she had of him suddenly resurfaced. She wanted to run up and hug him, but she was filled with mixed emotions. She turned around to look at her mother for approval because she sensed Janice would be uneasy. Cherry then turned away the moment she saw Janice looking at James at the corner of her eyes. Cherry never understood why he left and what on earth he was doing back there but she wanted to know, and she wanted to know everything.

She wanted to jump on him and hug him. Within herself, she also wanted to jump on him and *cuff* him in his face. As much as she was excited, feelings of disappointment and anger filled her. It was not the way she expected their first meeting would be since his departure.

She always felt like she would get butterflies in her stomach when she saw her father. She always imagined it would be an unforgettable experience where he would run towards her. He would wrap his arms around her, scoop her up and tell her how much he was sorry that he left.

As for Petra, she held back her tears. She wanted to tell her father how not being able to have a father to represent her on fathers' day for eight years hurt. She had so many questions for this man that was her biological father. She wanted to ask him all the questions she needed to know about him. She wanted to ask him why he abandoned them, why he abandoned her.

Likewise, in the same way, she wanted to tell him to go back from whence he came because he had no place there. After all, they were fine without him for the last eight years. Yet, all Petra did was stand next to her mother and remain silent. She glanced over at Janice and she could have seen her surprise and pain in her tear-filled eyes; however, that soon changed to anger. She knew that look all too well. They all did. They then stepped aside and let Janice be. No one was about to get in the way of Janice Hopkins when she was angry.

2. The Encounter

"What you doin' here, James?" Janice asked as she wiped her tears away from her face hastily. Her voice was raspy. You could hear it breaking with every word. It was almost as if Janice wanted to tell James off and break down in tears at the same time.

Yet, he never responded.

"James, ah ask you ah question." Janice said slowly, "What…are…you…doing…here?"

Janice was a naturally impatient woman. But at times, she showed a level of restraint that was outside of her character. There were times when she would give one a day to give her a suitable answer and there were times, she would only give a minute. Some days, no time at all. This time, her patience seemed to be dwindling quickly as she was not having James' silence.

Petra looked at Janice and thought to herself, that her mother was right to be upset. She had watched on as her mother waited years for this man to give her a reason why he had left her all alone to raise three children on her own. He was not dead. He was in San Souci, maybe with a new family. He was the only one with the full story and yet, there he stood, silent. So, she was right to be impatient. Her mother waited long enough and whatever trickle of patience was left, it was surely going away.

It was just about enough. Janice's chest began to heave and her nose began to flare like she was some kind of wild animal. For all the times the children had felt Janice's wrath, they had never seen her like this before. *Up. Down. Up. Down. Up. Down.* Her chest moved. Her eyes showed anger and she began to shake her hip, tapping her foot as she stared right at James. *Tap. Tap. Tap.*

She looked like she was some wild bull, those big black bulls seen on pastures with the big horns. She resembled that. Janice looked like Brown Boy, Mr. Joe's bull that he kept close to the ravine. Sometimes, JJ and Cherry used the path as a shortcut when they were heading home from school.

Mr. Joe's bull frightened Cherry because it always looked at them in an angry manner. It always looked like it was ready to charge. It looked like it laid in wait for the children, looking on with his devil eyes as he waited for the right moment when they passed to give them one hard *boot*!

But James was just staring into Janice's eyes, his words trapped; he just stood there in the veranda looking at Janice as she was about go to mad. Not long after, James finally opened his mouth as he looked down at his new brown converse.

And of all the things he could have said, James choose to ask Janice, *"Janice wha' you mean by dat?"*

"Look at you, dis no good man." Janice responded. "You have *the balls* to stand up in my veranda an' ask me what ah mean by dat?"

She paused. It almost seemed like Janice was gathering her thoughts to respond again. The tension could be felt between the estranged couple. The atmosphere was raw, almost as if Janice had practiced this speech over and over in her head or in front of the mirror. It was written all over her face that she had wondered what it would feel like to see James again and how she would react.

Janice let go of Petra's hand abruptly and walked full speed ahead to her residence. She climbed the stairs and stood face-to-face with James. She studied him – she looked down, then back up at his and said,

"James how much years you leave here an' never once look back? Eh James? Look how big you chil'ren is now! An' de problem is not that you go you know, you didn' walk out on me like everybody does t'ink. At least you tell me you was goin'. We had a plan. Me an' you sit down in dis same veranda an' we talk about it. You remember dat James? Eh? You remember dat?"

"Yes Janice, ah know." He stuttered.

"Oh ho. So you remember when you tell me dat the job you was gettin' was ah good one that could pay well? You remember how you tell me six months go go by fast, fast? Eh James? You remember how ah tell you hurry up an' come back an' doh leave me for too long with you two little girls.

Dey was not supposed to grow up without ah father, James. You leave here an' you didn' even know that ah was five weeks pregnant with you' son. You leave me with t'ree chil'ren an' you never look back. Not even a phone call, for almost eight years James! Eight?!"

"Janice, you doh understand." James interrupted.

"You damn right ah doh understand!" Janice shouted as she snapped back at him. "Right across de ocean dey you go an' not once you pick up the phone an' say you go give us a call. If you de throw a stone from where you livin' to here, ah sure it woulda buss me head. You ha' people comin' 'round to check to see if we okay..."

He interrupted her again, "But ah never ask nobody to..."

"Shame on you James! You never thought to do it for you'self. Da was too hard to do? Eh James? Da was real hard for you to do eh? What kind ah *waste-ah-time man* you is, James? Da is the kind ah man you turn out to be! Look, doh start me up here today about *no Janice what you mean by dat.*"

James hung his head and lifted it not long after. For a second, James looked into the eyes of his son; he could sense the pity and the shame. JJ looked away and started gazing around. James was somehow seeing that indeed, things had changed. He took his eyes off JJ and scanned the yard, until he locked gazes with Cherry.

She looked away, and the moment her eyes connected with Janice's, she knew their time in that yard had expired. It was time for them to leave *big people business* alone. Cherry was going to tell Petra that she should leave too, but the *cut-eye* Janice gave her, she knew that she should leave at once too. Cherry grabbed her eight-year-old brother by the hand and signalled to him that it was time for them to take their leave. They walked away, leaving James and Janice alone at the front of the house, attempting to sort out their differences.

Cherry wondered out loud, "what ah go call *him* now?"
Petra sucked her teeth and looked at Cherry at the corner of her eyes, but Cherry continued, "*James? James Sr.? James the first? Big James?* If dey have two *Jameses* around now, ah have to choose because I doh feel ah could call he *daddy* na."

For the two minutes she met him, Cherry felt like James' hesitance to give Janice some straight-forward answer lost him all rights to be called *daddy*.

To be a daddy meant that one had a relationship with his child or children. It meant that he was around when they needed him. Whether he lived in the same area or lived abroad, on good terms with his *child mudda* or not, a daddy meant that there was a bond that was existent. First impressions are lasting, and James did not seem like he cared that he missed out on eight years of all their lives.

~

JJ, Petra and Cherry walked all the way to the back of the house to avoid making contact with their father on the veranda. They took the back stairs that led to the kitchen. Because the door was locked from the inside, they had no choice but to all sit on the step and wait. There was complete silence. What could have been said to lighten the dampening mood that was now present in their home?

"Afternoon chil'ren."

JJ and Cherry turned around to see Mr. Joe heading to his house. He looked like he had just come from the garden. Mr. Joe had a routine; on Mondays, he would tend to his small garden at the front of his house, where he planted seasonings and flowers. On Tuesdays, he would go to the river to fish for *crayfishes* and *mullets*. Wednesdays, he considered his washing day. Thursdays were his days to clean his house.

On Fridays, Mr. Joe stayed at home and put his feet up. JJ and Cherry would always see him swinging in his hammock when they came from school. On Saturdays, Mr. Joe went to church in the Adventist congregation not too far away from JJ's old school, and on Sundays, Mr. Joe would go to the land to pick cocoa and nutmeg.

Mr. Joe was an unorthodox Adventist. He said that pork was the sweetest meat God placed on the earth and that God wouldn't punish him if he did not rest on Sunday.

When asked about it, Mr. Joe would always say, "Whether Saturday, Sunday, *Restday*, *Bessday*, ah go rest when ah feel like it. Papa God won't kill me."

Mr. Joe must have been about seventy years old. No one could ever quite tell because whenever people asked, he would say that he did not remember.

He once said to Petra, "Ah live me life ahready. Ah count enough years in me life. Ah closer to the grave dan de cradle. Ah en ha' time for dat ahgain."

"Afternoon Ol' Man Joe." JJ and Cherry said to him.

Mr. Joe stopped to look at them, then turned around, "Chil'ren chil'ren, wa do allu? Allu come out to church and allu lookin' so?"

"We good Mr. Joe." Petra responded with a look of annoyance on her face.

Petra was a force to be reckoned with. She was a private young woman who believed that her business was hers. She quite often said that unless she invited someone to be a part of it, that person had no right to know what was going on in her life. It was one of the reasons Cherry and Petra could never get along well.

One minute, they would be fine and she would be giving Cherry sisterly advice and the next minute, they were distant strangers. But it was undisputed that Petra loved Cherry despite of their differences; yet, she never showed it, and that was her problem. She never felt the need to publicly verbalise her emotions and feelings towards anyone.

"Ah watch allu grow up an' allu dey lyin' fa me?" They looked up to see Mr. Joe walking up the stairs towards them. "Chil'ren wa do allu? Wey allu mudda?"

Cherry swallowed the saliva that was growing at the back of her throat. She had never once lied to Mr. Joe, even at times when they had gone into his yard and stolen mangoes from his tree. There was no sense in lying to that old man because he always knew a truth from a lie. He often said that was a perk to living as long as he had.

"We fadda come back." JJ said as he broke the awkward silence brewing between them.

"Jamesy come back? Aa. Okay." Mr. Joe responded. "But how come allu siddung on dis step like somebody dead? Allu wasn' longin' to see him?"

Petra sat there in silence. Cherry too wanted to say something, but she was afraid that Petra would beat her up when they went inside. *If ah didn' invite you, ah doh want you in me business.* Cherry could hear Petra saying that to her as she punched her and pushed her into the partition that separated her room from Cherry's. Petra's business was Cherry's business now so she couldn't keep quiet.

Yet, Cherry felt the need to get the heaviness off her chest. She was overflowing with thoughts, questions she thought deserved answers and feelings she couldn't name. Cherry wanted to talk to someone, even if that someone was not her father. She wanted to tell someone how she *really* felt about her father's absence and his grand appearance. Although Petra wanted to remain silent, she too felt heavy and burdened by James' arrival, so did JJ.

Among the three of them, JJ did not quite understand the implications their father's return meant. The children sat on the step sorting out feelings of anger, confusion, happiness and disappointment. They needed answers and they needed to talk to someone who would understand.

"But..." Cherry continued, afraid that Petra would snatch her by her *picky* hair and drag her inside to put some licks on her. "But is not the same, Ol' Man Joe."

Mr. Joe sat down a few steps lower than the children and looked up at the three of them. He shook his head and gazed off into the bush that grew on the side of his house as he searched for his thoughts. No one said a thing. All that could be heard were the wind brushing against the trees, the gliding sound of the water in the ravine a few metres away, the birds chattering and Sammy's dog, Polo as he barked away.

"Ah know how you feel." Mr. Joe eventually responded.
"Ol' Man Joe, wha' you mean you know how she feel?" Petra snapped. "You fadda leave you fa years an' never look back? Eh? You doh know not'ing Mr. Joe. You doh know not'ing!"
"Aww Petra. Wa do you? You go talk to ah big ol' man like Mr. Joe so?" JJ said as he turned sharply to look at Petra. "You rude, wi!"

They were all confused and angry about the situation, but poor Mr. Joe. What did he do to deserve that disrespect? Janice always taught her children to respect the elders in the community. They had never disrespected anyone, especially not Mr. Joe. BrownsVille was that type of community where the village raised the children, so disrespecting someone else was like disrespecting one's own parents, and that did not happen at all.

"Ah go tell mammy about you!" JJ shouted.

"Leave her." Mr. Joe quietly responded. "She hurtin'. Give ha' she time to grieve."

Mr. Joe paused again, then said, "and yes Petty-gyal, ah know how it feel because it happen to me too."

JJs eyes grew wider and wider with curiosity. They had heard many stories from Mr. Joe, but this one was news to them. They never heard that tale before. JJ looked at Cherry intrigued by what seemed to be a new story about Mr. Joe. Cherry then looked at Petra for a sign of approval that it was okay to indulge in the conversation. But after a while, she did not care about her *rule* anymore. Mr. Joe never failed to deliver on a tale of his younger days.

Mr. Joe went through something they were experiencing that was new to them, so of course they wanted to know. Even Petra did but she did not want to seem interested. Cherry took her eyes off Petra and looked down at Mr. Joe in his garden clothes, with his nutmeg bag between his legs. He smelled like fresh mud when rain fell, and by that smell it was easy to know that it rained earlier in the mountains.

The skid mark on his back was an easy indication that Mr. Joe had either fallen once on his way up the hill or took a slide when he was coming down. By his foot, next to the *cutlass* that he carried, was a log. Its smell was easily identified as cinnamon or *spice* as it was commonly called in Grenada.

"Ol' Man Joe," JJ asked with no hesitation, "Wa you mean by dat? Wa you mean you know how it feel?"

"Well boy" he began, "Me fadda d' leave me an' me mudda too you know? E' was only when ah start to do good in athletics for Grenada in England, he come back aroun'."

Everyone knew Mr. Joe was an athlete who represented Grenada in the 50's. Mr. Joe was well known in the community, especially by the older people who were as young as Cherry and JJ when Mr. Joe was in school. However, no one knew about the story of his father.

The truth was, Mr. Joe hardly spoke about his father. He always spoke about his children, his mother, he once mentioned his wife but he never once mentioned his father. It was not hard to assume that he died when Mr. Joe was young.

As Mr. Joe continued to talk about the hurt he felt when his father came back into his life when he became successful, Petra looked up at Mr. Joe and couldn't help but listen; she was angry, but she could not resist giving him her listening ear.

~

Mr. Joe began, "Ah maybe d' just turn eleven an' me fadda pack he bag ah mornin'. He say he was goin' Petite Martinique (PM) on a farming project de government d' jus' start. Well dat is de story he tell me mudda an' dat is the one she tell me. De man leave from de time ah was eleven, an'

31

when ah d' jus turn seventeen an' was jus' graduatin' from Crownsborough Secondary an' get me firs' scholarship to go England for track an' field, he come back. Ah meet him in de house an me mudda say, 'Joel look you fadda.' Chil'ren, ah tell you *mad blood* bite me like red ants! Ah jus' walk out on him! He follow me an' he call out to me: 'Joe! Joe! Ah sorry ah wasn' dey before, but t'ings d' tight in PM so ah had to stay. Buh doh worry, ah make ah good bit ah money for all ah we. Ah proud ah you son. Ah real proud ah you. Ah proud ah de man you come out to be.' Ah move to England on de scholarship an' ah was makin' ah name for me-self an' makin' me country proud. While ah was up dey ah hear he was boastin' all over town about me."

Mr. Joe went on to tell the children that by the time he returned to Grenada, his father had moved back into the house with his mother. He and his father never got along. It was always a constant quarrel in the house. He said it was almost as if they were trying to see who had *the biggest set ah balls*.

Eventually, Mr. Joe returned to England where he married his wife, Cecelia. They had two children named Joanna and Cecil. Mr. Joe had not seen his parents for many years when he got the news of his father's death. It was a pain he said he never felt before. He could not understand how he could feel for a man he never knew. But he demonstrated to the children what a family bond was really like.

"It doh matter de distance," he said, "it doh matter dat ah-tall. All da does matter is dat is you family an' you ha' to love dem."

Mr. Joe continued to tell the children what it was like when he went to see his mother; he could not believe how broken she had become. Her smile was no longer there and her face was a bed of sorrow. No matter how much his father had hurt her, his mother never stopped loving him. She died only a few months after his father did.

Mr. Joe reminisced on the events leading up to her death and was persuaded that she died from a broken heart. What hurt most, he said, was that he never got a chance to reconcile with his father before he died. The day he left and never returned, his father put a serious licking on him for responding to him in a way he didn't like.

"He never d' like back-chat." Mr. Joe said, "An' ah use to have ah real sma't mout'. He used to always say dat *two cock can't live in the same fowl coop*."

Mr. Joe was convinced that there was no way a relationship that was *that* broken could ever be fixed. Mr. Joe was trying to be a man but even at twenty-four, his father still saw him as the same eleven-year-old boy he left.

Petra, JJ and Cherry sat in silence. Petra looked at Mr. Joe and she could see his eyes beginning to water. She felt horrible. They had never seen that man cry. He was human, yes, but he never showed any other emotion but joy. It was easy to often wonder why he was so different from all the other elders in BrownsVille. He was a wise man; yet it was not hard to see that his soul was once broken as his heart was.

~

"Ah say NO! No! No! No!" The silence was broken. It was Janice arguing with her estranged husband, James at the front of the house.

What could he have said to her that made her so riled up? Petra looked at her watch; it was the same watch James gave her on her twelfth birthday. *How ironic.* It was ten minutes to the hour of one o'clock. The children had been sitting outside for over an hour. The conversation between James and Janice must have been civilised up to that point because Janice sounded like she had about enough of what was transpiring.

James' silence caused JJ to think about the type of man his father must have been. *Ah wonder if he is ah aggressive man? Ah wonder wat about him dat make mammy like him? He does argue a lot? Ah find how t'ings lookin, he either real nice or real soft, maybe ah real washy-washy man.*

Mr. Joe got up slowly from the back step that they were sitting on. He picked up his cutlass, cinnamon stump he cut from the mountain, his nutmeg bag and said, "Chil'ren, chil'ren, ah go leave allu now. Ah ha' to put some provision on de stove to boil."

"Later, Mr. Joe." answered Cherry.
"Yeah, Ol' Man Joe, later." JJ seconded.
"Alright. We go see." Mr. Joe responded.
"Mr. Joe," Petra said as he made his way down the steps.

She was crouched with her knees touching her chest. She squinted her eyes to look up to Mr. Joe as the sun made its way from behind the thick white clouds.

"Ah sorry about earlier."

Mr. Joe chuckled then smiled, "Doh worry about it. Pettygyal, all ah we does get a little mad blood too, ent?"

She smiled, "Yes, Mr. Joe. Later."

Mr. Joe walked down the stairs and opened the gate at the bottom of the stairway. He leaped over the drain that separated his boundary from the Hopkins'. He walked towards his small concrete house and picked *a hand of fig* from the tree bearing adjacent the building. He inspected it and placed it in his bag. He walked slowly up his back step until his figure disappeared.

The children immediately began to dissect Mr. Joe's story. They discussed what they heard before from neighbours who knew Mr. Joe and compared it to his account. To them, it captivated a side of Mr. Joe that no one saw. The children continued to ask each other questions, until Janice opened the door that had been bolted from the inside.

"Come an' take out allu food" she said.

She made no mention of what transpired or where James was, and the children were wise enough to not question her about it; that was grown folk business.

Cherry thought to herself, "*lemme leave dat big people business for big ooman Petra, who feel she could raise she voice for ah big ol' man like Mr. Joe. Wait 'til mammy hear about dat. But me, ah en go tell her. JJ go tell mammy 'cause ah know he like to run he mouth wen he ready. Not me."*

Janice always said that Cherry spent too much time preoccupied with Miss Millie and her antics. She began to gossip excessively, but she would never admit that she did. She always felt like JJ talked too much. Janice warned Cherry that she brought too much news on other people, and if she was not careful, one day, someone was going to bring news on her too. Since then, Cherry tried her best to cease being a tattletale. Janice's words seemed more of a curse than a warning.

Petra pulled the door open and JJ and Cherry walked in. Petra stayed behind and went back to sit on the step. It was evident on her face that her thoughts were overwhelming. Tears could be seen forming in her eyes and she didn't want her siblings to see, especially Cherry.

Cherry then turned around to see her older sister looking troubled. She did not know what to do. It was true that she couldn't tolerate all of Petra's ways, but she was the big sister; the always tough big sister who never seemed to let others see her weakness. However, like Mr. Joe said, *all da does matter is dat is you family an' you ha' to love dem.*

It was so different to see her looking so dismayed, and she really didn't want to, but Cherry turned around and asked, "Petra, you go be okay?"
She nodded at Cherry and Cherry took that as the sign to give her sister some space.

No one knew what this new dynamic would do to the Hopkins family. Things were changing, and no one knew if this change would be for better or for worse.

3 Daddy Visits

It was 5:45am when Cherry woke up the next morning. The sun had not yet risen. The breeze blew her peach curtains high into the air. She could hear the distant chirping of the birds as they were on their merry way to find food and some sticks to build their nests. The dogs barked, cicadas screeched, and cocks crowed.

Since Petra's persuasion that the morning was the best time of the day, Cherry decided to follow her sister's routine and wake up early too; she loved it! She enjoyed indulging in nature. Somehow, the air smelt different than it did on busy mornings and later on in the day.

Cherry laid flat on her back staring at the ceiling. No amount of nature and persuasion could get her out of bed that morning. What happened yesterday was too much to ignore. It bombarded her thoughts and left lots of unanswered questions. *Wey daddy was for all these years, and why now of all times he come back? Mammy en make him stay, so ah wonder wey he go? He maybe dey by Uncle Donté.*

Seeing her father now was nothing like she imagined. She always thought it would be a happy experience; James would be happy to see her and she would be happy to see him. He would hug her closely and there would be lots of tears and kisses. But James only looked at Cherry for two seconds when he saw her before he looked away.

Cherry turned over to the other side of her bed to see two fat mosquitoes resting on the partition that separated Petra's room from hers. She could never understand how the mosquitoes got to suck her blood in the night when she ensured that she was covered from head to toe, with a fan blowing in her direction. She slowly turned over to pick up the bible that was at the side of her bed. She turned over again to see that one mosquito had discovered her plan and flew away. However, the other one was still resting on the partition.

Gradually, she lifted herself off the bed frame then struck the mosquito with the bible armed in her hand. **Splat**! Instant death. The mosquito was crushed in between the partition and the bible. Half of it stuck to the partition and the other half to the bible. Blood was spread over the wall and a tiny leg could be seen wiggling its final moments until it had given up the ghost completely.

Yes! Ah get him. Cherry thought.

Cherry got up and headed to the bathroom for a piece of tissue to clean up the mess that was made, and as she walked down the hallway to the bathroom, JJ's door was left ajar. She peeped in to see him fast asleep. The entire house was quiet. Today, Petra was not up early, and it certainly was not like Janice to wake up after any of her children. Today must have been one of those days. Cherry took the toilet paper, returned to her room and wiped the remains of the mosquito off her bible and off the wall.

"Good morning!" It was Mr. Joe walking at the back of the house, heading towards or from the ravine. He paused then began to say, "It doh good…"

Before Mr. Joe could finish, Cherry pushed her head through the window and responded, "Ol' Man Joe, morning. Yes, it doh good to make de sun get up before you."

"Cherry-oh, you takin' ol' people advice these days. Dat is good. Have ah nice day you hear?"
She smiled, "yes Mr. Joe. Have ah nice day too."

Cherry sighed and knelt down beside her bed. Before she went to bed, she asked God to give her some answers. She wanted all the questions she had answered and she wanted it answered now.

"God, thank you for de day today, for my family an' my friends an' for all your blessings. Today, I ask that you give me my heart's desires and direct me in the intended path you have set out for me. Bless my family, wherever they are and whatever they are doing. Be with us all as we go through dis day. In Jesus name I pray with thanksgiving, amen."

~

Unlike JJ, Cherry never really liked school, but Janice always said it was foolish children that did not want to go to school. Cherry knew she was no fool, so she went every morning the doors were open. Whenever she attempted to pretend that she was sick so that she could stay home, Janice would say,

"Cherry, you playin' you like to cry wolf! You gettin' on like Bobby and dem boys up de road dat fake sick until dey never go ah day to school. You know wey dey end up now? On de streets smokin' weed an' beggin' people for money."

Bobby was Janice's cousin. His father's name was Henson, and Henson's mother was Gertrude. Gertrude was Janice's aunt, making Henson her first cousin and Bobby her second cousin. Bobby grew up in the small community of Consent. Bobby now lived alone but when he was Cherry's age, he lived with his grandmother, Matilda.

Cousin Matty, as they called her, was too much of a lenient woman, in Janice's opinion. Janice always said that her refusal to discipline her grandsons made them walk all over her. Eventually, cousin Matty died of a stroke. When she died, Janice cried, "is dem good-for-not'ing gran'sons she ha' dey dat kill her wit' stress!"

To avoid having Janice use Bobby as a reference in her life, Cherry complied and went to school. The teachers said that Cherry was an average student and with application and the right encouragement, she could do much better. But Cherry thought, no matter how much she tried, she could never go past that *average* mark they were always talking about.

She enjoyed some subject areas more and worked as hard as she could on them. She liked to write a lot, but strangely enough, she was not an avid reader. It was not that she didn't do it, she just was not as fond of it as she was of creative writing. She also liked Social Studies and French as a foreign language. Chemistry was interesting to her but not any of the other sciences. There were some things about Math that piqued her interest but nothing else about school excited her.

Cherry still tried her best to focus in school and study hard. She got to school early, she did her homework on time, participated in school and extracurricular activities. Cherry tried to be as respectable as Janice Hopkins would want her to be and she made all attempts to not drag her or her mother's good name through the mud.

Before congratulating her after she passed her Common Entrance exam, Janice said to Cherry, "When you go in dat school dey chil', doh make me shame!"

And that is what she tried her best to do - to not make Janice shame.

With that, Cherry stayed away from the delinquent students in her school. She didn't have much friends, but she got along with almost everyone she interacted with. She never had a best friend but Danisha was the person she was closest with in the school. Danisha had a best friend of her own who was in form five, a form higher than theirs. Cherry gravitated to Danisha because of her positive qualities. She was smart, friendly, caring and honest - sometimes, just a bit too honest.

Danisha lived in Morne J'adore with her mother, father, younger sister and older brother. She travelled from Morne

J'adore to La Baye every day for school. Morne J'adore was located at the north of the island, La Baye at the southeast and BrownsVille at the east. How Danisha was able to travel to school every day, on time and sometimes even earlier than the students who lived in La Baye, no one knew.

At the La Baye Presbyterian School, the population of girls outweighed the boys. Both Danisha and Cherry were not fond of the few at the school.

"Ah never see more *jahpah* boys in me life dan ah see in dat school." Cherry would tell Danisha.
"Ah know gyal." Danisha would laugh. "Who go like dem? Early morning? Smelly. School uniform? Jahpah an' smelly. Attitude? *Tusty*!"

With that deportment and Janice's constant reminder that *books and boys doh mix*, Cherry never got herself involved with any of the boys she came in contact with.

It wasn't that she had what old Grenadians would refer to as *unnatural tendencies*, she had seen boys in movies and around that she found attractive, but she never got into practices she knew her mother would not approve.

Quite often, Cherry heard people in the community talk a lot about the sweet words some of the young girls in the village fell for, but not Cherry. She never had the chance to hear them because she was too afraid to stay around boys long enough for anyone to see her. She was always afraid that someone in the community would see her and report her to Petra or Janice.

When she was in the second form, there was a boy named Grayson that she had really liked. She never knew if he liked her because she never had the courage to tell him and he never told her how he felt. If ever there was a chance of expressing her feelings, that was flushed down the toilet when her classmate Seanda got pregnant. Cherry feared that she would have the same fate and heeded her mother's advice.

Seanda was fourteen at the time and lived in Charlestown, a community a few minutes away from BrownsVille. She lived with her 26 year old sister Kim and her sister's boyfriend, Lucky. Her mother Gail died of complications due to AIDS and Seanda never knew her father. With a lack of proper parental supervision, Seanda was left up to her own devices and got involved with Danny, the neighborhood *village ram*, and the rest was history.

~

Math on a Monday morning was like giving JJ ochres to eat; it was hated. But on this day, the class were continuing simultaneous equations and that was an interesting topic to Cherry. It didn't change her mind about Math, but at least it kept her interested in the subject for the double-period class.

Mr. Wilkinson was the fourth form Math teacher. He was in his early forties and had an Associate's Degree in Advanced Mathematics. He always claimed that he had a passion for Math but you could never sense his enthusiasm. In Cherry's opinion, he was a very boring teacher. That might have contributed to her disinterest in the subject.

"Now class," Mr. Wilkinson said as he dragged his words as slowly as he trailed the number 167 across the board with the stick of chalk. "Let us turn to page one hundred and sixty seven."

Cherry sank into her chair and folded her arms. She loved the topic but she just wasn't feeling like engaging in her Math class today.

Why ah really come to school today, boy? Cherry thought to herself.

She sucked her teeth under her breath; soft enough so that Mr. Wilkinson didn't hear but at an equally elevated level so that the students around her could hear her protest. She sat up and stretched her body in front of the desk. She let out a long, exhausted sigh and pulled out her workbook. She opened the book. Page 139. She turned to page 140. She flipped and flipped page after page in her workbook. *Wa do Wilkinson in truth?*

Page 167. She read the instructions in her mind: *Solve the following simultaneous equations using the example given below.*

"Students," Mr. Wilkinson said in his slow, annoying voice. "please ensure that you have rechecked your answers before submission."

Cherry picked up her pencil and scanned across the room. Everyone was already with their heads buried in their workbooks, except for her. She looked down at the first question and began to work as her mind wandered through the events of the previous day. Before long, the sound of the school bell could be heard across the classrooms. Cherry had spent the last few minutes day dreaming.

Pling pling pling pling pling pling.

The quarter to twelve lunch-bell had buzzed through the halls of the La Baye Presbyterian School and the students were pleased. As Mr. Wilkinson struggled to maintain the order in the classroom for the last few seconds that he thought was his, half of the entire class had already made their way to the corridor. Some raced to the lunch line to buy their lunches, others who ate at home, raced to the gate.

Mr. Wilkinson knew very well that he was no match against the famished children, so he took out the stick of chalk again and began writing on the board:

H/W

Complete the equations from page 167 - 168. This should be handed in at the end of the week.

~

"JJ!" A voice called as he walked out of the La Baye Junior School gate. The primary school was adjacent the secondary school that Cherry attended. It was half past two and school was finally over for JJ. He really wanted to get to the field for football practice. A lot had been on his mind, but he was glad when he turned around to see his sister Cherry sprinting towards him.

"Aye. Ah goin' football practice." JJ said as he turned to his sister.

"Ah know." Cherry responded to her younger brother. "Mammy say to pick up de shoes by Mr. Broke-oh for her when you finish."

Mr. Sanderson, or Broke-oh as he was called, was the shoe maker in the area. He lived close to the field where JJ and his club would have their practice. He was referred to as Broke-oh because of the way he walked. His ligaments and joints were permanently damaged when he contracted the Poliovirus during the outbreak in Grenada, in the 70's.

JJ assured his sister that he would not forget and headed to the field with their cousin, Jumario. As Cherry watched JJ walked towards the field, Danisha came up from behind her and asked, "You doh goin' home?"

"Yeah ah was jus' passin' on ah message for mammy. You know how JJ head hard; you does have to tell him t'ings twice for him to remember, wi."

The girls laughed as they walked out of the school gate and unto the main road, two a-breast. Danisha looked at Cherry and without hesitation asked, "So how come you never tell me you fadda come back home?"

Cherry did not respond but kept on walking alongside Danisha. How did her friend who lived all the way at the north of the island hear the news of her father's return before she had a chance to tell her, herself? Leave it to Grenadians to spread news like wildfire. Cherry wanted to talk to her friend, but she didn't feel the need report her father's return to anyone.

"Who tell you da?" Cherry inquired.
"Well, ah de hear Marina tellin' Suzette she mudda say she see him down by Black Boy shop dis morning."

Marina McBurnie was a fifth form student, and if making another person's business her own was a subject, Marina would pass with flying colours!

"She say two ah dem used to go to school together back in de day." Danisha continued. "So how come you never tell me?" Danisha asked again. "Ah say we d' good."

Cherry looked at Danisha and responded, "Well he show up yesterday but ah doh really want to talk about it."
"Why?" her friend asked.

Wa do dis girl in truth? Cherry thought to herself. "Because e doh really ha' not'ing to talk about. Ah neva even get to talk to him when he come because he and me mudda d' dey quarreling whole time."
"Okay. Ah know how it does be." Danisha lied.

She did not know how anything *does be.* Danisha had a mother and a father who had to have loved each other because they were living together and had been doing so for over twenty years. She had a little sister who looked up to her and a big brother who protected her. What exactly did Danisha know?

The girls walked up the road in silence. Cherry was bothered by her friend's response but she was not in the mood to start arguing with the one person she was close enough with to consider her friend. Cherry eventually let it go. When they got to the main road, the pair walked passed Busy Corner until they got to High Street. Danisha was heading to the bus station so Cherry decided to pass by her mother's office.

"Well ah dey if you want to talk to me." Danisha said as they stopped at the Morne J'adore bus stand in the town of Brussels. "Ah going an' see if ah could catch de bus. Me uncle come out from England yesterday. He have a barrel for us. Ah go bring some chocolate for you tomorrow."

"Alright, later." Cherry responded.

Cherry cut through St. Mark's Street which was just after the Brussels Police Station. She headed to Pen Street where her mother worked. Janice worked with the Ministry of Social Services as a Social Worker. She had done so for the past twenty-three years.

Sometimes on her afternoon walk from school to home, Cherry would pass the long route through the town to get to BrownsVille. She would pass by Janice to see if she wanted her to carry any bags home. When she arrived in the office, Janice handed Cherry two bags; one contained grocery and the other contained fish. Janice instructed Cherry to clean and season the fish before she got home.

Brownsville was just outside the town of Brussels. It was about twenty-minutes' walk from La Baye to BrownsVille and

Cherry didn't mind. However, on days when she left school late on evenings or just didn't feel to walk, Cherry would take the short route from La Baye, through Walkerson Trace to BrownsVille.

That day, Cherry decided it was best to walk, that way she could clear her thoughts before she got home. She walked to the end of Pen Street and took a left unto BrownsVille. Not too long after, she was walking unto Conch Street. She stopped to talk to Sammy and to give her daughter Phoebe a kiss. She liked Phoebe. She was a real pleasant baby. Phoebe didn't cry much and loved to laugh. Sammy said that she took the day off because Phoebe's babysitter was sick. They talked for a little, then Cherry made her way home.

~

Cherry said good afternoon to everyone she passed, as was customary. When she got to the house, she could not believe what she saw. It was her father sitting on the veranda again. What was she going to say? She wondered how her mother would feel if she found out that Cherry was talking to James when she was not at home.

"Afternoon." Cherry said as she stood in the yard like she was a stranger.
"Afternoon Cherry-oh." James responded. "Watch how de girl get big."
"Yeah." Cherry responded.
"So wa de gyal say?" He asked with the typical Grenadian line when one didn't know what else to ask.

"Ah dey." Cherry responded with the typical generic response for that typical Grenadian line.

"Okay." He said. "How school goin' girl? We have a lot of ketchin' up to do, eh?"

"Yeah." she said again. "School goin' good."

"So wey you brother an' you sister?" He asked

"JJ dey in de school still. He had football practice today an' Petty gone to work." She glanced at her father then looked down.

"Aa. Me boy like he football like me. An' wey Petty workin'?" he questioned.

As soon as she heard him ask about Petra, it was almost as if Petra stood behind Cherry and whispered that reminder into her ears, "*If ah didn' invite you, ah doh want you in me business.*"

"Well mammy finishin' work for five so you go ha' to come back to see her." she said as she tried to change the topic.

"Well," he said as he stood up. "Ah was hopin' ah woulda see allu today but is jus' you. But ah bring a little thing for allu. You go put it inside an' tell you mudda ah sen' it. Is just some little groceries an' t'ing for you, you brother an' you sister."

James sported a red polo shirt and grey denims. He had a red cap on his head and black and white sneakers. Cherry looked at her father; he was a very handsome man and he was well dressed too. She wondered where he was off to or where he was coming from. Was he all dressed up to see them, or maybe in the hopes of seeing Janice?

"T'anks." She said as she came forward to take the bag from James.

"You han' done full ahready," he said. "ah go rest it on de chair here for you. Ah going up de road. Ah hope to see allu again. We have a lot ah talkin' to do."

"Okay. Later." Cherry responded as she looked at her father take his descent down the five-tread step. She stepped aside and watched on as he walked out the yard and up Conch Street.

Cherry walked up the stairs and picked up the bag of groceries her father brought. She dropped the bags her mother had given her and began to open the bag James left with her. Cheese. Milk. Two boxes of frosted flakes. Four cans of Pringles. A large packet of sausages. Three tins of corn beef. Two parcels of shop bread.

James seemed to have taken his time to choose some of the things he knew the children would like. She thought that the gesture was considerate but to her, it wasn't his get-out-of-jail-free card. She hoped he did not expect that from that one bag his wife and children would come running back to him, especially not her.

Cherry took out her keys from her school skirt and opened the front door. She picked up the bags she had dropped earlier and entered the house. She dropped the bag of fish into the bucket by the kitchen, placed the two bags of groceries on the table and headed for her room. She changed from her school uniform into some comfortable *home clothes* and headed back into the kitchen where she began to clean and season the fish.

It was Dolphin. She loved the taste of Dolphin; it was her favourite fish. She liked red fish too, but she had too many bad experiences with the bones sticking in her gum and at the back of her throat.

Cherry couldn't eat jacks; she was allergic. Janice would say that Cherry ate too much of it as a child. As a result, her body was now refusing it. Whenever she ate it, her mouth would begin to experience all sorts of uncomfortable changes: her lips, throat and cheeks would itch and shortly after, her throat would begin to swell. On a few occasions, Cherry had to be rushed to Dr. Nelson's office where she had to be given an allergy shot to reduce the swelling.

After Cherry finished with the fish, she headed to her room. She looked at the time; it was 4:15 pm. In a few minutes, Janice and Petra would be coming home from work. Petra worked as an accountant with Mr. And Mrs. Churchill whose office was on Yellow Street. Petra had been working there for two years. It was her first job after graduating from TAMCC where she attained her Associate's Degree in Office Administration. Petra enjoyed school unlike Cherry. It was her desire to attain her BA in Business Administration.

Janice always encouraged her children to pursue an education. She reminded them of the struggles her parents went through to send her to school and always told them of the benefits she was able to reap. Petra had no intentions of furthering her education but before long, she saw the importance. It was her hope that Cherry would soon change her view on her studies.

Cherry switched the television on and turned to channel forty-five. *CSI: Las Vegas* was now playing; it was her favourite TV show. The episode airing was one she had already seen but she looked at it anyway. She liked to see how intently Grissom worked at getting to the bottom of each case.

"Afternoon Cherry." She turned around to see Petra coming through the door.

Cherry looked at the clock to see that it was nearly an hour later.

"Afternoon." She responded.
"Mammy come home ahready?" Her sister asked.
"No, nat yet." She answered.
"And wey JJ?" Petra asked as she took off her shoes and sat on the couch beside her sister.
"He ha' football practice today." said Cherry.
"So wa you watchin' dey girl?" Petra asked as she unbuttoned her blazer.
"CSI." Cherry said, "Dats the one we see wey dey bury Nick an' de ants and dem bite him up."
Petra laughed, "Yes girl, ah de like da one."

The girls sat on the couch and looked at the episode until it came to an end. It was a quarter to six o'clock and they could see Janice walking down the dirt path to her home. By the time she reached door, Petra had already gotten up and gone to her room to change her clothes.

"Good afternoon." Janice said, "wey allu brother?"

"He have football practice today." Cherry responded.

"At dis hour? Da doh done yet?" Janice asked as she looked at the clock.

"He maybe go an' pick up de shoe for you by Broke-oh an' go by Uncle Donté wit' Jumario, ah sure." Cherry interjected.

"Okay." Janice said as she walked towards the kitchen. She was carrying a hand of green bananas that she placed on the table.

"Cherry," she called. "Nat de fish you have on the table dey? Chil', ent ah tell you clean an' season de fish for me so ah could cook it when ah reach?"

"Aww, mammy, no!" Cherry protested. "aww, ah clean de fish an' season it ahready. Ah put it in de fridge!"

"So wa is dis next bag da dey on de table dey?" She asked.

Cherry swallowed hard. Her heart thumped almost as if it wanted to jump out of her chest. She was so preoccupied in CSI, she completely forgot about the groceries James left for them. After their confrontation the day before, Cherry wondered how Janice would respond to him coming around, especially when she was not at home. Cherry did not know what to say. Maybe she could just pretend like she did not hear her. Maybe she would think it was from Miss Donald and forget about it.

"Girl you doh hear ah talkin' to you?" Janice asked. She put her bag down and proceeded to open the grocery bag James left with Cherry.

"Who bring dat, Cherry?" She asked again.

"Daddy give me dat when ah meet him here today." She nervously responded.

Cherry glanced from the corner of her eyes and waited at the edge of the couch to see if the bag would come flying across the dining room, through the living room and out the front door.

"Hmm," Janice said. "So he come here today?"

"Yeah, when ah reach home, ah meet him on de veranda." She explained.

"So wa he come an' do here?" Petra added.

"He say he come an' look for us." She reported.

"Stupes!" Janice sucked her teeth. She pushed the bag of groceries to the other side of the table.

Janice took the bunch of bananas, placed it into the sink, picked up her workbag and headed to her room. As she walked to her room, she could be heard mumbling and quarrelling under her breath, "James doh ready yet."

4 W'en Ah Ready

A few weeks after James' visit to his estranged family, the Hopkins discovered that he was living in Sandal Bay with his cousin Donté. Miss Millie had mentioned it to Sammy who told Cherry. Eventually, Cherry shared the news with Petra, who told her mother and her brother, JJ. Leave it to Miss Millie to know.

Uncle Donté, as the children referred to him, was not James' brother, but his first cousin. It was imperative that all children refer to their cousins more than fifteen years older than them, as uncle or aunty. Donté was tall and extremely handsome. His well-built figure coated by his dark chocolate complexion was a quality the young women could not resist. Donté and James grew up together in BrownsVille.

When they were younger, people often thought that the boys were brothers. That's how life was on the island. Brothers were brothers, younger cousins were brothers, older cousins were uncles and the persons who one referred to as cousins were either *pumpkin vine* relatives or more than likely, never related.

Donté was a contractor with PJ's Construction and Masonry Operations. His father and James' father were twin brothers. The men never produced a twin of their own and that is why it was always thought that Donté and James must have been brothers. Their bond was special, and wherever one saw Donté, more than likely, James was there.

Donté was married many years ago and around that time, he lived in Charlotte Bay with his then wife, Margaret and their son Jumario. Any blind man could have seen that Margaret and Donté were not right for each other. Only two years into their marriage and after the birth of their only son Jumario, Donté and Margaret parted ways.

Compared to their rocky togetherness, their separation was surprisingly peaceful. They did not hate each other; they just knew that they were better off being co-parents than a couple. Donté left the house in Charlotte Bay with Margaret and Jumario, and moved to Sandal Bay where he built a new home.

He never dated anyone but he was also never single. Just like Danny, Donté was considered the village ram, a senior village ram. Whenever talk of Donté came up, people were always surprised that he only had one son.

Unlike Danny, who had dropped his seed in almost every corner of the island, Donté only yearned for a woman's company for a moment; the next, he was gone. He boasted that no woman could give him a *jacket*, because he always used protection.

He swore that he could never fall in love with another woman, but he could not do without their tender touch. It was that one thing that made James very different from him.

Donté never recovered from his broken marriage but James loved Janice more than she knew.

Donté loved Jumario; he made all efforts to visit his son as much as his work schedule would allow. He frequently took his son fishing in *Humble Pride*, his ten-year-old fishing boat. Donté bought the boat the day he and Margaret finalised the divorce. To him, it was a symbol of freedom and letting go of the past. He once said that stepping on his boat and riding out into the deep ocean made him view life differently. He saw the ocean as his safe haven; it was his place of refuge.

When Jumario was eight years old, his father brought him for a ride on the fishing boat. Jumario always said that he wanted to be a fisherman, but his parents never wanted that life for him. Donté discouraged Jumario from wanting to become a fisherman, since he lost his own father in a boating accident when he was only sixteen years old. Donté was never the same. He wanted to ensure that he was around for his son for as long as he lived.

"Ah not goin' to bury me son like how ah had to bury me fadda!" Donté frequently said.

Jumario always felt like his father never wanted what was best for him, but it didn't take him long to realise it was quite the opposite. A year later, nine year old Jumario decided that he did not need his father's company anymore to travel on the sea. Yes, the island was surrounded by water, but there were dangerous parts that required adult supervision. Even so, a nine-year-old had no right on a boat without his guardian.

Soon, he lost control of the boat and was thrown overboard. What was even harder for Jumario was his inability to swim. It so happened that Donté was not too far behind when Jumario took off. He rushed into the water and swam out to him. Donté could see Jumario being pulled into an incoming rip current. He made the decision, that if he had to sacrifice his own life, he would do so just to save his son.

Thankfully, no one died. Donté was able to save Jumario and bring him ashore. Donté however, was so distraught, he put a serious licking on his son to warn him about the seriousness of what he did and that he should never do such a thing, ever again. Jumario got the message, because he never pulled a stunt like that, and he never once questioned his father's love for him.

~

Donté returned home to find James swinging comfortably in his hammock. It was after three and James had not kept to his promise. It was the decision of *the boys* that if James had to stay with Donté for the time being, he had to find a job and contribute to the home.

The fact that James was home at this particular time, probably meant that he made no attempts to find a job or his attempts were again, unsuccessful. He was a contractor by trade and it was one of the reasons Mr. Samson hired him for the job in San Souci. As Donté stood in his yard looking at his cousin, fast asleep, he began to reflect on James' life just before he left for San Souci.

James was excited about the job opportunity. After speaking to Mr. Samson about the duration of the job and the necessities to get it done, James got advice from Donté whose opinion he valued greatly. Donté initially did not agree with James' decision to go but later took his cousin's word that it would be a much-needed opportunity to better himself and his family.

Donté appreciated the CSME certificate James had, which gave him and all islanders in the Caribbean the opportunity to work throughout the isles. However, he felt that San Souci, in particular, was not a place for his cousin to work. There had been many stories of the high influence of *Obeah* on the island and the tales of men who were trapped into leaving their families and staying with strange women in San Souci.

"You know how much ah dem man an' dem from mainland da go up Souci an' doh come back? You want to give Janice hell, James?" Donté initially said to him.

It took Donté a lot of convincing for him to agree with his cousin's wishes. Although James had a job in Grenada, things were slow. It was the main reason his boss, Mr. Samson, decided to send him on the six-month contract with Blonders and Co.

Donté walked up the stairs, one step at a time. His walk was slow-paced, hitting each boot hard on the step so that James would be startled and wake up from his slumber. James did not flinch. *Thump. Thump.* No movement. Donté looked at his cousin and sucked his teeth.

"James!" He hollered. James groaned but he did not open his eyes.

"James!" Donté called again as he jabbed his cousin in his side. James quickly opened his eyes and squinted them to initiate facial recognition of the handsome muscular man that stood before him.

When James could recognise his cousin, he sucked his teeth and sat up, "Eh, Dono wa you do da for? Boy wa you want?"

Donté looked at James and shook his head, "Boy ah tell you dis is not ah hotel. Ent ah tell you you ha' to try an' get ah wuk? You cyah live here for free, James. Things not as good as dey used to be boy. If you have to stay here, ah need ah little help."

James struggled to sit up comfortably in the hammock, "Ah hear you de first time Donté. Ah went by Mr. Delores dis morinin' an'…"

"Who is Mr. Delores?" Donté interrupted.

"Mr. Samson used to work with Mr. Delores when ah jus started to work with him." James responded. "Anyway, ah meet him de other day an' he tell me anytime ah lookin' for ah wuk ah must call him. So ah went by him today an' he say he have ah contract comin' up next week but jus' for a fortnight."

Donté breathed a sigh of relief and sat in the chair opposite his cousin, "Ahrite, well dat good. Papa God shine He face on you."

Although he really needed the financial support to feed the one hundred and eighty-seven pound man who had moved into his house, Donté was happier for James because he could see the frustration and sadness in his eyes. Every morning he woke up feeling irrelevant and depressed with the thought of being so close to his family, yet so far away.

Added to that, James had revealed to Donté that there was a reason why he could not leave San Souci and it was an explanation even he would not be able to grasp. Donté's imagination brought him to places he had never been before as he struggled to understand what mess his cousin could have gotten himself into.

Because of his guilt and fear for James' life, Donté religiously visited Janice to ensure that she and the children were well cared for. He even, at times, put money into her account in the pretence that it was from James.

Donté never quite understood why James never called Janice and he felt that it was his duty to ensure that he was the middleman between the two. He loved the children. He treated them like they were his nieces and nephew, and not like if they were just second cousins. He especially looked out for Junior, as he would call him.

Donté felt like he had to play the role of a father figure in the boy's life since he never had the opportunity to grow up with James. He understood even so, how his own son felt when he separated from his ex-wife Margaret; he never wanted JJ to go through the emotions his son did. It did not matter whether James was alive and living on the other island, the fact that he was not present in the home meant that the boy would lack something.

Donté took JJ swimming, fishing and on his farm lands with him and his son Jumario. JJ might have only been eight, but Donté ensured that JJ and his son Jumario learnt every trade there was to learn from him. He would occasionally remind them that depending on the government to find a job for them to provide for themselves and their family, was meaningless.

He would say, "Dr. Primus an' he people an' dem in power never had anythin' good to offer allu. Santrock an' he boys now is de same thing. Learn ah t'ing or two from what ah does be doin' an' you doh ha' to worry about goin' wit'out."

~

Donté was not politically inclined, but he kept current with everything that had happened and was transpiring on the little island of Grenada. Prime Minister Otis Santrock was a humble man, but Donté felt like he was not right for the Prime Minister's seat. However, Donté was of the opinion that Santrock was far better than former Prime Minister Primus Bedeau. He was of the opinion that Dr. Bedeau had engaged in some ungodly practices, in hopes of maintaining his political seat.

No one could confirm whether the rumours were true, but they never subsided. It wasn't until people began coming forward to confirm said rumours, that Dr. Bedeau decided to give up his seat and retire from politics.

Many people from Petite Martinique and mainland Grenada claimed to be eyewitnesses of a situation which took place in August 1988, approximately twenty-seven years ago. While Bedeau, then leader of the opposition, held a rally in the South-west constituency of Grenada, several gun shots rang out at the opposite end of the island. Not long after the evening's proceedings were over, a breaking news clip was aired, where it was confirmed that then Prime Minister Franc Lewis was assassinated.

His driver had just pulled his car up to the side of the stage where he was about to exit the vehicle and walk towards his political platform. He had arranged an impromptu political meeting with his constituents to personally deliver some "breaking news". Before he could do so, he was murdered. Shots rang out through the small village of Homestead and the people grew frantic. His wife Portia and deputy leader Martin Levi were both present when he died.

As those present in the rally scampered, the police officers who were at the rally scouted the venue to find the gunman. Their search was futile, but the apparent weapon used to kill the Prime Minister was found discarded at the back of the field. A few persons who were witnesses to the assassination claimed to know the man who had done the crime. They were most certain that it was Kenneth Thomas, a drug user in the area. It was not long until he was picked up, and after heavy interrogation, Kenneth confessed to the brutal assassination of Prime Minister Lewis.

What was even more shocking was his claim that then opposition leader, Dr. Primus Bedeau and his political team, were the masterminds behind the crime. Dr. Bedeau and his party denied all claims and maintained their innocence throughout the ordeal. The young man was eventually sentenced to death. Upon his final statements before he was hanged from the gallows, Thomas pronounced severe curses upon Dr. Bedeau and the entire Democratic Reformed Party (DRP) if they did not accept responsibility in Prime Minister Lewis' death.

Too shaken up to stand against the DRP, deputy leader Martin Levi stepped down from his post and the Grenada Democratic Union (GDU) was dissolved. In the upcoming election, Dr. Bedeau was voted in and appointed Prime Minister of Grenada, and the country was never the same; it was almost as if everything he touched was destroyed. The country faced a hard time under his ruling. One by one, each one of his cabinet members began facing serious illness and even death.

Some claimed to see Dr. Bedeau and his cabinet members receiving *bush baths* from prominent voodoo priests and Obeah workers in Grenada and on the island of Petite Martinique, claiming to ward off the evil spirits assigned to them by the young man who was executed. When questioned about the new claims of his charms and protection spells arose, Dr. Bedeau denied them. However, as quick as Prime Minister Bedeau denied, more and more people came forward to speak against him.

Eventually, the convicted cabinet members brought the situation to light and on their death beds, they confirmed that the rumours of the bush baths and protection spells were true. Yet, they were silent when asked about the assassinated prime minister. Dr. Bedeau resigned as Prime Minister, leaving the country in the hands of his deputy leader, Dr. Susan Miles, and moved to Florida to live out the rest of his life. It was his hope that he would escape the wrath of the Grenadian people. Eventually, Dr. Bedeau died in an unfortunate hit-and-run accident. To this day, no one stepped forward to accept responsibility for his death and his confession died with him.

~

"Ah meet Denis de other day by the water plant," James said interrupting Donté's wandering mind. "He say he havin' ah cook down by him weekend. Wa you sayin'?"

"Yes ah dey in dat. Wa we ha' to bring?" Donté asked.

James got up off the hammock and stretched his long arms, "He say he want to make ah crayfish waters an' he want us bring de meat. Ah find we should go an' trap some crayfish like ol' times."

"We go go Friday night," Donté responded. "De moon en out; is de best time."

Donté got up off the chair in the veranda to join his cousin on his feet. The men walked to the front kitchen door and entered like they were visitors; they wiped their feet on the mat at the door and proceeded towards the living room. As James sat on the couch and picked up the remote, Donté sat on the sofa opposite him and looked at his cousin. James looked up at Donté and knew that he had something on his mind.

"Boy, wa happen?" James said in a tone that signified his annoyance. "Wa you want now?"

"Ah want to bring Jumario with us when we goin' Friday to trap crayfish." Donté said.

James looked at him, "Okay? So, since when you does ha' to ask me to bring you son on t'ings you accustom doin' wit' him?"

James kept his eyes fixed on Donté; he knew that there was more to that statement, but he could not figure out what else there could be.

Donté shifted in his seat and rocked forward as if easing in closer to tell his cousin a deep, dark secret, "Ah want to bring Jumario an' ah want to bring Junior too."

James looked down and his eyes froze on the carpet that ran from the kitchen to the hallway. It laid as an object of separation between them. His eyes were fixed on a stain that had to be beer from the night before. James was clumsy; he had spilled his beer while looking at the Football games on Grenada and the Grenadine Isles Television (GGTV). He kept staring, in an effort to distract himself from the issue at hand - his son.

It has been over two months since he returned to the island and beside the occasional brief visits, James had never gotten a chance to sit down with JJ. It was an awkward feeling for James. It was only when JJ was seven years old that he contacted Donté who told him of his son's existence. It was one of the reasons Donté felt obliged to be there in the boy's life, because he knew his father would not or could not be there.

"So you go jus' sit down dey an' look like ah *beh-bel-joe?*" Donté asked as he stared at his dazed cousin.

Stupes. James sucked his teeth and rocked back into the softness of the couch. "Ah doh know. Me an' de boy barely know one another. You doh find da go *funny?* What if he doh come? Ah doh fine na."

Deep down in his heart, James longed for a relationship with his son. The very first time Janice got pregnant, James wished for a boy. By the time Cherry was born, James lost all hope in ever having a son as he and Janice had planned on only having two children. However, that did not stop him from loving his children immensely.

When he got the news of his son's existence, James knew it was the only reason Janice had kept the news of her pregnancy from him. It was an unplanned pregnancy. He deciphered that in her mind, if his job had run its six-month course, she would have surprised him with her pregnancy upon his return.

"James," Donté said, "dat is ah good time to get to know de boy. All four of us as man doin' t'ings as ah family. Ah does bring him with me and Jumario all de time. Just let de boy come na man."

James paused. He searched in his mind for a good-enough excuse why this meeting would not work, but he couldn't find one. "Well okay," James said, "but if t'ings doh work out good, doh blame me."

"An' if he doh come, ah won't blame him." Donté said as he looked at his cousin wallowing in his own regret. "Because ah yet to hear what happen in Souci an' how come ah could count de amount ah times on one hand ah hear from you for de amount ah years you go."

Without looking at his cousin, James picked up the remote and turned on the television, "Ah tell you when ah ready, ah go   talk   to   you   about   it."

5 James & James, Jr.

"So, he go be dey?" JJ asked.

He looked across at the waves beating at the beach front, and gazed off into the distance. The man had not been in his life for a single day but was showing up out of the blue now and requesting bonding time. According to his Uncle Donté, he, Jumario, JJ and his father had a hunting trip on Friday. It was always a tradition for the three of them, but now, they had a plus one - his *long-lost father*, James.

Donté looked at JJ as he focused on the Caribbean Sea waves that calmly approached the shore. He could feel the ease as they came forward and withdrew; he wished his feelings within him were as calm as the waves. Donté could sense the tension that brewed within; yet he did not say a word. He allowed JJ to feel what he was feeling because he could have only imagined what he was thinking not only of his father, but also of himself.

When JJ was four years old, after a short boat ride with his uncle Donté and cousin Jumario, JJ turned to his uncle and asked him the unthinkable: *"Uncle Donté, why me fadda doh want me?"*

He looked at his uncle with great concern in his eyes. Donté was lost for words; he did not think that at that age, the boy would have accounted his father's absence to a fault of his. It took a lot of explaining and convincing to help JJ see that his father loved him despite his absence. Although Donté for himself could not give JJ a reason why his father had not yet returned, he hoped and prayed that James would return soon for the sake of his son. JJ oftentimes felt left out as he was the only one in his household who had never met his father before two months ago.

"Ah doh know." JJ finally responded, "Me an' de man doh know each other. You doh find da go feel *funny*, Uncle? What if he change he mind ah he doh come? Ah en sure na."

Donté could not help himself but laugh out loud when JJ had finished his sentence. It was the exact excuse his father had used days earlier. Donté knew the pair could not be more alike. He just wanted them to see how much of a great relationship they could have if they only got to know each other a little.

"Wa so funny, Uncle Donté?" JJ asked.

"Like father. Like son." Donté responded as he tapped the boy on his shoulder still chuckling. "But doh worry about it Junior; he comin' and ah hopin' you go come too. Is ah nice time for you to see de kinda man you fadda is."

"Well alright. If you say so. Ah go see you later. Ah ha' to go in football practice."

"Alright me boy," Donté said as he knocked JJ's knuckles, giving him a *bounce*. "We go see."

~

Cherry was sitting on the back step reading the final chapter of *Cat & Mouse* by James Patterson, when her mother opened the back door. She looked up to see her shaking her head as she looked at her daughter.

"Cherry, ah sure you doh do you' homework yet." Janice said. "Ah could bet *me bottom dollar* on it."

"Afternoon mammy." Cherry said as she closed the thick book she was engulfed in. "Ah goin' an' do it now. Ah almost finish de book; jus ah few more pages lef'."

Janice shook her head again, "Hmm. Chil' ah doh know wa to do wid you again. But at least you teacher doesn' have to be callin' me to tell me you not studyin' you school work. Better dat dan you down de road studyin' man like Seanda. Make sure ah doh ha' to ask you again for de evenin' to do your homework eh, Cherry."

"Yes mammy." Cherry answered as she hurriedly flipped through the final pages of the novel.

Cherry did not like to read, but of late, her discovery of James Patterson's novels captured her attention. She spent more and more time each day digging into his thrillers. *In Cat & Mouse*, Cherry was about to discover who the killer was. As Cherry read, she was stunned to discover that the detective who was assisting in the criminal investigations was the actual serial killer.

Adrenaline pumped through her veins as her eyes widened at the discovery. It was indeed a case of *cat and mouse* between the law enforcers and the serial killer. As the story concluded, Cherry took a few seconds to revisit the vivid images of the characters that were painted in her mind. She thought about the victims and how they felt when the last images in their minds before they were brutally murdered were those dark eyes behind the killer's glasses. What a horrible feeling!

Cherry got up from the stairs and stretched her tired legs. She looked over to her neighbour's yard to see if there was any sign of Mr. Joe. It was 5:30pm on a Wednesday afternoon and Mr. Joe's laundry was swaying in the cool breeze that blew.

Quite often, he would be in his veranda reading his newspaper or listening to the radio after his laundry. Today, he was nowhere to be found. It was quite a natural occurrence for Mr. Joe to find his hand in something else, as he could never sit still.

Cherry opened the backdoor and returned to the inside of her home. She walked towards the stove to see if any food was left back for her to eat. Whenever JJ passed through the kitchen, it was almost as if a starving pauper had visited.

As she took the lid off the metal pot, she could hear her mother shouting, "Make sure you wash you' hand dey eh!"

But there was nothing in the pot, so Cherry walked to her room to do her homework.

A few hours later, Petra walked through the door and dropped her frame unto the beige sofa. She greeted her mother and sister. No one answered; their eyes were glued on the tv screen. It was the 7:00pm news on the other local television station, National News Network. The headlines read:

BREAKING NEWS: MAN MISSING FOR TWO MONTHS FOUND FLOATING IN ARANIA BAY.

The silence in the living room was deafening. The island was peaceful and there were hardly any murders that took place. While neighbouring islands would have 500+ murders at the end of the calendar year, Grenada would have less than five. It had been the talk of the town that Mr. Baron was kidnapped, and his body parts sold on the black market in Central America. Others claimed that he had drowned the same day he went missing, but his body was never discovered.

However, no one was of the opinion that Mr. Baron had abandoned his wife and family. That accusation did not suit his personality. He was a friendly man who loved his family; every job he had done was to ensure that there were meals on the table to provide for them. There was no way he could have left them.

Janice sighed a heavy sigh. It was one that needed no words. She felt pain. She felt pain for Mrs. Baron who had lost her husband, because many times before, Janice had wondered if the day would come when the news of James' death would reach her. There were times when a sliver of hope overshadowed her, nudging her on to keep the faith - her husband was alive and well and would soon return. And there were times that she felt that all hope was lost.

Janice had stopped anticipating James' return the day JJ had turned two. She lost all hope. Her husband had promised that in six months he would have returned. Yet, it had been two years after, James was nowhere to be found. Deep down, Janice anticipated James was alive, but if he was not, she prayed he was buried somewhere where he would find rest.

However, years later when the money began filling up in her account, she suspected that her husband was very much alive. She was of the opinion that he had found a new family and started a new life; unfortunately, his sympathy money was not going to satisfy either her or her family.

"Goodnight." JJ said as he walked through the front door.

It was now 7:05pm and the darkness of the night had settled over BrownsVille. The tall, muscular, soon-to-be nine-year-old JJ walked into the living room and stood looking at his sisters and mother. It was hard to believe that he was only eight. He had matured faster than the other boys in his age group and often looked like he was in his early teens. It was something Donté told him his father had experienced.

Janice leaned forward to look at her son, then she glanced at the clock over his head. "Ah fin' you coach an' dem playin' de beast wit' de long ears, JJ. Dat is time for dem to be sendin' people chil'ren home?"

Janice paused, "watch de time! Doh leh me ha' to talk to dem eh because you maybe look like ah big man but you not one yet."

JJ shook his head. He dropped his sporting gear on the floor next to the sofa. He knew very well that he was not allowed to sit on the beige suede sofa after a long evening of football practice. His mother frequently reminded him of how hard she worked to earn the money that paid for the sofa. She customarily added that it wasn't *his father's sorry money that paid for it.*

JJ attempted to always avoid all conversations that had to do with his father, but that night, he wanted to strike a conversation about him. It was something Janice would never expect and also something she dreaded. However, the conversation about his father tonight did not trigger those kinds of emotions.

"Mammy, ah see Uncle Donté an' he ask me to go an' trap crayfish wit' him tomorrow…" JJ's sentence was incomplete but his mother could not tell. She was lost in her own train of thought.

"Alright." She responded without looking at her son.

"Ma, Uncle Donté say is de four of us da goin'." He said as he looked hard into the direction of his mother. "He say me fadda go be dey."

Janice, Petra and Cherry lifted their head as the sound of the word *fadda* escaped the lips of the young boy. Petra looked at Janice, and Cherry glanced at her mother's expression in the corner of her eyes. Everyone was silent. Even JJ. It had been almost three months since James had returned, and his presence was not yet welcomed.

Two entire months had passed and he had not given a proper apology nor explanation for his disappearance. It was never Janice's intentions to keep her children away from their father but over the years, it seemed as James wanted nothing to do with them.

"You fin' ah should go, mammy?" JJ asked, breaking the dense silence that had settled over them.

"Is whatever you choose to do, wi." Janice answered as she rolled her eyes and struggled to get out of the couch she had sunken into. "Ah doh stoppin' you from seeing you fadda."

Janice walked towards the kitchen. She put her cup into the sink and headed towards her room. The children could sense the tension that had built up within her at the mention of James.

~

Petra graduated from the T.A. Marryshow Community College at the age of seventeen, with an Associate's Degree in Business Management. She was employed that same year by O&S Churchill Limited, as an Accounting Clerk. She was fortunate enough to be employed a few days after her graduation, unlike the hundreds of graduates in Grenada alone that remained unemployed. Things were slow on the island, so any opportunity for employment that arose, young people were encouraged to take it.

Petra enjoyed working with Mr. Oswald and Mrs. Shandra Churchill. Their accounting firm had begun to bloom only four months after her arrival. For many years, the Churchills had suffered a loss in their company because they had not a fresh pair of youthful eyes to assist them in their business. Many of the techniques used by the couple was quite outdated, and they suffered at the hands of dishonest employees who weaselled their way into their finances.

Petra worked with a young man named Json Frederick, who was the senior accountant in the firm. Json had graduated from the University of Accounting on the island of Antigua about five years prior. Jay, as the Churchills referred to him, moved to Grenada from Antigua two years prior to assist the Churchills. Mrs. Shandra, his grandaunt, begged the assistance of her grandnephew in the family business. With the aid of Json and Petra, the Churchills were able to regain the good name their business once had.

However, on this particular day, Petra could not keep focused. She had struggled all morning to get out of bed and she was struggling to complete the simple tasks that were given to her. *Recheck the Bragg's account. File the new Johnson account. Prepare the monthly report for Mr. Frederick's review.* The day could have been a short working day if she could just do what needed to be done.

Yet, Petra was somehow distracted by her own thoughts. She fought within herself to come to grips with her father's return; however, her lack of emotional expression had not afforded her the opportunity to express to her mother or siblings how she really felt. Petra was well known but she did not keep many friends. That in itself was a recipe for disaster. It was the reason for her occasional sudden outburst.

It was 10:17am; it had been one hour since Petra sat at her desk rechecking the Bragg's account. She was physically present but mentally absent. Physically, she was at her desk rechecking the Bragg account for the umpteenth time but mentally, Petra was at home under her sheets or in the ravine behind their house taking a cool morning dip.

Her father had returned and she had not yet seen him. He visited her mother. He visited her sister. He was making plans with her brother, but he has not inquired about her. Maybe she had been right all these years; maybe she was the reason he left.

A tear poked out of the corner of her tear duct and attempted to roll down her rosy chocolate cheeks. Without even knowing it, Petra was weeping at her desk as her mind wandered to her absentee father. It was until Json had approached her, Petra realised she had been crying – out loud! There was no pretending this time. The *I'm okay* and the *it's nothing* could not suffice for the explanation Json frequently requested.

"Petra, I'm not sure what the issue might be and it's okay if you do not want to talk to me, but you will need to talk to someone." Json said as he leaned over her desk. "I'm a good listener, but I will respect your wishes if you do not want to talk, but please, talk to someone else. It's been two weeks since you've been disheartened. Whatever it is, I trust that it will all be well soon."

Json waited for a response and when he thought that he would get none, he was about to walk back to his desk. In no time, Petra broke down crying. It was not like her to let others see her emotions but this time, there was no silence or filter on what she needed to express. The years of pent up anger and frustration began to come out.

Her emotions got the best of her and Petra let herself cry. She had held back her emotions for too long. This time, she was going to set herself free from the emotions that she had held unto. The conversation exceeded an hour but Json did not seem bothered. He wanted to understand what Petra had been going through. He had tried many times to *read* her, but her walls were well erected.

Now he knew; behind the strong-willed personality and her desire to always bury herself in her work, there was a young girl missing the love of her father. There was a thirteen-year-old girl who waited for years for her father's return but he never came. There was a broken young girl who wanted her father's love and the comfort of her mother.

Json felt the emotions Petra had felt and with a soft tone, he said to her, "You have to let him know how you feel."

Petra looked up at Json with red swollen eyes, abused by her tears. She shook her head to reassure him of the fact that she understood. Json did not say a word but he sat there with her and silently said a prayer.

~

"Afternoon Miss Millie." JJ said as he passed Miss Millie's gap to head home. He kept his head straight, avoiding all eye contact with her. JJ had thought about getting home to look at *Seven Deadly Sins* all evening. At the end of his class, it was announced that football practice was postponed, so he rushed out the school gate without waiting for Cherry. He was most certainly not about to let Miss Millie cause him to miss his show.

Miss Millie was a talkative old woman who always felt like no one was too busy to listen to her complaints or have a nice conversation with her. She felt like she was obligated to talk and anyone who crossed paths with her had to be committed to listen.

"Chil' wey you runnin' to go? De house doh goin' no wey!" Miss Millie shouted out to JJ as he made a run for it.

JJ laughed as he ran up the stairs leading to the veranda. He was lucky today to escape the blabbering mouth of Miss Millie. For an old woman, she was very strange. She oftentimes reminded JJ of the old witch Tabitha in the show *Passions* his mother Janice liked to watch. Just like Tabitha, Miss Millie kept most of her business to herself but was somehow always in the know with the affairs of others.

It was 2:58pm. JJ took the last two minutes he had to rush to his room, change his clothes and put away his bag before Cherry came home. He knew when she did, she would rush for the remote. By the time he did what he had to and got back to the couch, the recap had already begun. JJ's eyes were glued to the T.V until the episode was over. He breathed a sigh of relief when he discovered Meliodas was alive!

Not long after, JJ heard a male voice outside. It was his father. He wondered what he would do to avoid him. He was afraid. His uncle Donté recently told him that his father would join them on their hunting trip. JJ looked through the louvers to see his father standing in the yard like he was unfamiliar with the house.

In a sense, he respected his decision to not barge into the home that he once called his own. There was still unfinished business between Janice and James and it would be a shame if he had entered without his mother's permission.

After much deliberation, JJ opened the front door and stepped out unto the veranda, his heart thumping heavily in his chest. JJ stood in front the door as James turned around to see his son. JJ wondered what his father was thinking as he stared at James and James stared right back at him. He looked across the road to see Miss Millie suddenly inspired to clean the windows that was facing his small home; the same window she had not cleaned in years.

"Good afternoon." James said as he fumbled for words.

"Afternoon." He responded.

JJ wondered what he would say to his father and from the look of things, his father may have been wondering what to say to him. For a few seconds, the two just looked at each other without saying a word. He imagined what it would be like when he spoke to his father, yet this experience was confusing. Deep within himself, JJ felt compelled to ask his father many questions but the fear within him kept him from doing so.

James looked at his son and said, "You look like me, in truth."

"Oh." JJ responded. Again, his desire to continue the conversation was halted by his fear that he would say the wrong thing or say something to upset his father. He longed for a relationship with him but he did not want to show him how he felt.

JJ could see the disappointing look in his father's face when all he had to offer to the conversation was *oh*. But what could he say? He hadn't a clue. The silence between the two of them grew thicker and tense. It was awkward to feel the tension that built between them.

Not long after, James said, "well ah jus' pass to see how allu doin'. Ah goin' back up de road."
James told his son he would see him later and turned to walk down the stairs. "Well you go tell Cherry and Petty ah pass, eh?" James said as he struggled to hide his disappointment.

JJ nodded but he felt bad. James made the effort to visit him and that must have counted for something. Before James walked away, JJ stepped out of the front of the door and said, "ah go see you Friday."

James turned around and his face lit up like the lights on the houses in Grand Pines that were decorated at Christmas. He nodded at his son and went on his way. Before JJ went back inside the house, he looked at his father walk up the dirt path from Conch Street. As he disappeared along his journey back to Sandal Bay, Miss Millie conveniently disappeared from window-cleaning duties. JJ went back inside the house and sat on the couch, thinking about what transpired. He could not wait to tell his sisters when they came home.

6 Bonds will be Bonds

"Boy you de right, wi." James said as he turned to his cousin. "Ah woulda regret if ah didn' go with allu de other night."

Donté smiled without responding to James. He knew that he made the right decision in not cancelling the trip they had planned. As he sat listening to the enthusiastic account of James, he reminisced on the night *the boys* had gone to the Homer Great River to hunt for fresh water crustaceans.

Crayfish was a delicacy on the island, especially for those living close to rivers. It wasn't an easy task hunting for them; it was one that required skill and precision. Donté and James frequently visited the river when they were young boys and often lived on river food.

The younger boys were trained by Donté on the right way to fish. When it came to mullets, their fishing tools were made from plastic bottles, fishing line and a fishing hook on the end. It was a trick Donté and James learned from Mr. Williams who lived not too far from where they grew up.

The hook was tied with a double knot to one end of the fishing line and the other end was placed on the inside of the bottle, wrapped around the neck of the bottle and the cover screwed on. The excess line was wrapped around the body of the bottle.

When it came to trapping crayfish, a bait was set and secured until the crustaceans found their way to the traps and were caught. Another way the crustaceans were caught was with a fishing rod made with fishing line and bamboo. A *cacadoh* was placed on the end as bait for the hunted crayfish. Both required a high level of skill and patience, both of which Mr. Williams taught the men. James had been familiar with the waters and went ahead setting the traps. It was dark outside and he had to be careful. After several traps were set, they waited.

James took the opportunity to talk to his son. It was the first, real conversation he had with him since he caught a glimpse of him months prior. For a man in his late thirties, he was not immune to the fear of rejection. He always wanted a son, and there was the young boy, his son, sitting on a few stones away from him.

He pondered on what he was going to say before he summed up the courage to talk to JJ. He did not want to seem forward, but he also did not want to seem shallow. Donté was dicing the avocado he had brought as bait while JJ and Jumario were *ol'-talkin'*. James carefully walked back to the spot where the boys were.

"What allu talkin' 'bout dey?" He asked. A slight tremor accompanying the words as it escaped his lips.
Jumario looked up, "We de dey talkin' about de football game da go dey."

James looked at JJ who did not look up at him. His son seemed uninterested in engaging in a conversation with him, so he contemplated retreating.

Just then, a voice said, "Ah hear you used to play football for we school too." It was not Jumario but his son, JJ.

Football was a topic that both had interest in and it was easy for them to get engaged. James had been a star player for the Grenada Football Team and assisted them in several of their victories. JJ, like Miss Millie always said, was the copy of his father. His interest in and love for football was just as his father's was. As they shared their stories, agreed and disagreed on teams and players, JJ eventually let his guard down and opened up to this father.

As the three talked and laughed, Donté occasionally glanced in the corner of his eyes. He was pleased. He was happy that James had gotten what he always wanted - a son to call his own, one whom he loved and was beginning to love him. They fished, they hunted and the evening was well spent.

~

James sat uneasily on the chair opposite Donté. He felt that it was time. The man had practically taken him into his home and did not complain a single day he was there. Fear gripped him and it was clearly on his face, because Donté had put down the remote he was aimlessly holding and turned to James.

"James, wa goin' on wit' you?"

James clearly heard Donté, but he did not respond. For one, James was very much afraid of the consequences that were before him if he revealed the truth about his stay in San Souci. It started off as a wonderful opportunity that he took advantage of. He took the time to call Janice every day and speak to his daughters. At nights, James would cry as he missed his family dearly.

As the first month went by, James held on to the hope that he would see them again soon and that the money he was making would be able to get them out of the financial hole they were in. He turned to Donté who was still looking at him with an expression of concern on his face. He started to tell his eight-year long story.

"Mr. Samson move me one day." James started.
"Mr. Samson move you one day? Wa da mean? Wa you talkin' about James?" Donté eagerly questioned.
"Come na, man!" James shouted, "You ask me to tell you what happen so ah tellin' you, but you ha' to give me time too. You find da easy to talk about?"

Donté retreated. He knew James was serious.

James was silent for a minute and started to share again, "He move me to work on dis house in Fort Dale on the country side. He say dis ol' lady was renovating a litlle *Janet house* she had dey. De pay was more an' de time was shorter. All ah was t'inkin' about was Janice an' de chil'ren, so ah went.
De first day ah go dey, ah didn' t'ink anybody was livin' dey until dey tell me about dis ol' lady livin' on de en' ah de

streeet da does never come outside. Ah never see her for the firs' few days but ah always use to say good mornin' an' good afternoon. Mr. Samson show me dem t'ings an' it look like it woulda take two weeks to do 'cause he sen' me dey me alone.

Ah never pay attention to dat boy, like ah tell you, all ah was t'inkin' about was me wife an' me chil'ren. Boy ah was workin' with pace because ah done count it down in me mind, two weeks an' ah goin' home. Ah wanted to surprise Janice an' de chil'ren 'cause dey would'a never expect me to come back so quick."

James stopped and shook his head. It was the first time he would tell the truth about his experience in San Souci. Many people suspected that he was nothing but a cheater. They claimed that he had left his family and started a new one. Even Janice eventually fell into the trap of believing the lies. But how could she? She knew James well enough to know that that didn't fit his personality. She had known him for years; he was the kind of man to always tell the women he was a married man, *married to one wife and in love with her.*

"De firs' day ah go up dey was me an' Mr. Samson." James continued. "It didn' have nobody dey so we stan' up on in de yard an' decide how ah go get de job done. De house was ol'. It look like it stand up dey for about ah hundred years. Mr. Samson wasn' sure why de lady didn' want he advice to jus' break down the same parts she wanted to keep. But she was de one payin' so he didn' fuss."

"How far was de place from where you was stayin'?" Donté asked.

"About half an' hour drive an' ah hour walk from de house Mr. Samson had us in. It was real far from all de other houses in the area. Ah know because ah try to walk to work ah day when de van wasn' workin'. Ah get ah ride from ah man an' he bring me up."

James continued, "the firs' few weeks was normal; I never t'ink t'ings woulda turn out how it was up dey."

Donté was fed up of the suspense and blurted out, "oh gosh, jus' tell me wha' happen and done na! Chuhts man!"

Although annoyed, James knew Donté was right. The fear of his cousin's response and the idea that he could be called crazy if the truth came out was blocking him for a long time from being honest about what really happened in San Souci.

Added to that, James knew Janice would never believe him; so he kept the account to himself. But as he thought about it, the truth was the only thing that could set him free from the mental chains that had him bound for so long.

"Ah day ah went to finish de las' piece ah work ah had to do in de back of de house. An' it look like ah stumble upon somet'ing she didn' want me to see. She had a whole shrine in de back ah de house. Voodoo doll, candle wit' people name on it, bible turn upside down, cow foot, chicken foot an' a lot ah blood, everywhere.
Me papa, you never know me to eat and drink t'ing from people so ah was glad ah never accept anyt'ing from her. Ah decided to leave before she realise ah was in de back dey but

when ah turn around ah see she standin' behind me wit' some kinda stick in she hand. She blow some kinda dust in me face an' start to chant some foolishness.

Me head start to spin and is like de whole place was movin, except me. She curse me right dey an' she tell me ah go never see peace in me life again. Ah run out dey quick an' is like ah screamin' but nobody hearin' me."

James took a deep breath and continued, "from the night ah go an' sleep cous', ah start to see all kinda t'ing. The first night, ah dream ah was on the sea on ah little boat and de ol' lady stan' up on de water waitin' on me while ah oarin' the boat. Ah get up 'fraid 'fraid cous'. Ah en lying to tell you, ah nearly pee de bed. Ah was so 'fraid to get up.

De next day, ah go to work to tell Mr. Sanderson ah cannot work wit' de lady no mo'. He tell me if ah want de money ah ha' to finish what ah start, so he sen' Johnny to come an' help me. Ah finish quick an' went home. Ah try to pack me stuff to leave but all how ah try, ah can't do it. The night come now an' same dream. Ah in de boat oarin' out an' the ol' woman jus' stand up dey waitin' on me. For t'ree nights, ah dream de same t'ing."

"An' how come you en tell Janice?" Donté interrupted.

"Ah try to but ah didn' want to frighten her! You know me to keep t'ing from dat woman, you self? But ah jus' couldn't. But me an' Janice pray de night but it like not'ing en happen. She pray wit' me the next day ah had to go to work, we talk an' is like not'ing change."

Donté sighed, "so wa happen next? Wa happen so to have de woman worried for all these years. Ah mean ah know you call me an' talk to me all these years after an' sen' little money, but something was off an' ah could'a tell."

The concern on Donté's face grew more and more. He knew that James was not a bad father and the most loving person he could be to Janice. He knew also that his cousin, although understanding, was not a man to stand for nonsense, so the idea that a woman would come between him and his family was something he knew James fought hard to overcome.

"De next time ah notice t'ings was gettin' outta hand was the las' day ah had to work. By dat time, ah ask Mr. Sanderson to transfer me back to the original work site ah was on. Remember ah tell you two weeks alone we had to be dey? The last day ah finish all ah had to do an' all ah t'inkin' about was that Janice would'a real glad for me to be home early. An' ah really wanted to see me girls too. Ah de really miss me family, boy."

James' eyes trailed off as his mind began to float into the past. Donté was unaware how best he should react, so he sat in silence, waiting until his cousin was comfortable to share again.

"So de las' day ah work now in the evening time, about 4 o'clock, the las' finishin' touch had to do an' Jimmy didn' come. Ah finish all ah ha to do an' ah was in the yard packin' up me tools. Dono, all ah was t'inkin' about was Grenada, me family, me wife. Before ah could realise, ah feel me head spinnin' an' ah gettin' bad feelin' an' dat was the las' time ah was in me right senses, wi."

James relived the moment he realised he was spiritually chained by what seemed to be an Obeah woman. He had noticed many things before but one night, James lost control of himself; it was the beginning of a spiritual cycle he could not free himself from on his own.

~

The wind blew through his small room. It was 2:30 a.m. and the night's *coldness* began to settle in the air. No. Not the cold temperature one would feel that would make one's body shiver. The cold feeling that could be felt in the soul. He turned around to see the long flowing white dress hoovering over his window. It was happening again, and he couldn't help the pull he felt towards her.

As she hoovered away, he trembled. Fear gripped him in a way nothing else had startled him. He told Donté of the moment he wanted to tell Janice what he was experiencing, but it was almost as if he couldn't. No matter how hard he tried, the words could never come out clearly. He told Donté of the moment he thought about Janice's temper and how quickly she would think he was just making the perfect excuse for having another woman.

"Is true boy." Donté interrupted. "Da wife of yours doh easy, na."

James laughed to himself as his gaze fixed to the corner of the room. Many times, he had the opportunity to tell Janice what was happening, but he was so scared his truth would cause him to lose her. Somehow, even his secrets still did.

James continued.

At 3 a.m., he was awoken to the feeling of the strange presence in his room. It was the similar feeling he had earlier while on the phone with his wife. He rose off the bed – eyes bright and blazing; he was in a trance, *again*. He walked towards the window, crawled through the opened space and planted his feet on the wet grass. It was cold, but he didn't feel it. His eyes were glued on the beautiful young woman, adorned in the white long dress. It was night but the young woman's head sported a big straw hat that covered the majority of her face.

He walked towards the bushes right ahead of the San Souci Great River and was lost behind the trees that overlooked the flowing water. As the woman stripped her clothes and entered the cold water, James did the same.

And as it happened, in times past, at the break of dawn, James would wake up at the mouth of the river, lost and confused. He would have to search for his clothes and make his way back to the house. He felt embarrassed, confused and violated. What had happened? Why couldn't he remember? And worse yet, why wasn't *Papa God* listening to his prayers to stop this woman from taking advantage of him? He had planned that morning to leave the island as his last work day was the day before. One way or the other, he was getting out of that place and never returning.

"Boy, remember ah tell you about dem stories ah hear? Dat is why ah didn' wan' you to go dey. Ah sorry to hear dat but you ha' to tell her, man!" Donté exclaimed. Eyes bright from fear of what he had heard and the thought that Janice should know the truth.

"Ah real worried, boy. Ah worried she go call me a liar an' she wouldn' believe me." James said.

"Liar?" Donté questioned. "Papa God know you heart. You get tie to ah La Diablesse! She could say wa she want, . Is better you give her dat dan not'ing at all."

James shook his head in agreement. He knew, for once, his cousin   was   right.

7 Ah Wan' to See Daddy

Janice sat on her brown leather couch in her room. She often stood over the couch hugging tightly around James' broad shoulders. As she sat alone that evening as she did many evenings before, her mind played on the recent events as it usually did. She missed James. She had missed him for the many years he had been gone but she knew if she made it known, people would think she was crazy.

A lot of the ladies in the village often speculated that Janice had already moved on and spent all of her time with her new beau outside of BrownsVille. Miss Millie, on the other hand, was known to tell the women that Janice had *closed shop*. Leave it to that wretched old woman to "know" everybody's business.

As she sat alone on the couch positioned in front of her king-sized bed, Janice began to cry. Her sobbing was bitter, but silent. For many years, she cried alone in her room. Oftentimes it was her fear that her children would come to console her and desire to know what was wrong. Many times, it was the answers she didn't have that frightened her the most – especially with Cherry.

From the time she was born, she was a curious soul. Cherry frequently asked why. Janice reminisced on the times James would grow wary of the question;

"Oh gosh chil'!" He would exclaim, "you doh tired?"
Then a four-year-old Cherry would ask," Tired? Why?"

Janice laughed to herself as she wiped the tears away. Cherry
was the light of her father's life. He had no favourites; he
loved his daughters just the same. While Petra was serious
and focused, Cherry's personality lit up the house. As Janice
thought about the years past, she remembered the moment
James left for his job in San Souci.

She remembered how much the girls cried, especially Petra.
Petra loved her father with a love unending. It broke her
heart for him to leave and it broke his heart to see her cry.
Janice remembered having to pull Petra off her father at the
Carenage.

The Osprey was about to leave. Martin, the doorman and
ticket collector called out to James, "James-o, doh ha' dem
people waitin' so, boss."

James embraced his wife for the last time and kissed her
passionately. He wiped away the tear that was trickling down
her cheek and looked down at his daughter, sobbing
miserably. He looked over at Cherry who was standing
quietly at her mother's side.
"Behave allu self. Doh give allu mudda no trouble. And
you," James said as he took Petra by the hand, "stop all da
cryin' dey, you hear? Ah go see allu later."

As James stepped onto the ramp and handed Martin his
ticket, he looked back at his family for one last time, blew
them a kiss and walked into the ferry.

"Daddy!" Petra shouted, "ah want me daddy!"

"Chil' stop dat dey!" Janice snapped, but her harsh tone only made Petra more frustrated, and her whining and wailing escalated. "Watch gyal! Stop cryin' before ah give you somet'ing to cry for! You doin' like if you fadda doh comin' back!"

As Janice remembered the words she told her daughter and James' reassurance that he would be back, she hated herself a little. But how could she foresee that James would not keep his promise? How could she know that he would betray her...*or did he?*

~

Petra and Cherry walked up the gravel road and called out to their uncle. Since his return, Petra had not seen her father. James had stopped by on a few occasions to bring goodies for Cherry, but he was never lucky enough to see Petra. Since their *crayfish trapping* session, James and JJ had spent lots of time together. It seemed like the son he never knew he had turned out to be the son he loved dearly.

Petra had summed up enough courage to call Cherry after school to ask her if she would accompany her to see their father. Cherry knew that it had to be serious. Petra always seemed like she could handle everything on her own; however, since James' return, she seemed vulnerable. The pair met in Brussels at ten minutes past four.

Cherry told her mother she was going to meet Petra to help her choose some fabric for a work suit. *She lied.* Janice had been so out-of-it since James' last visit, she didn't even bother to question Cherry further.

On a good day, she would say, *"who little boy you goin' an' meet down de road an' puttin' you sister name as cover-up?"*

But today, Janice just said *alright* and let Cherry go. The girls chattered for the entire five-minute ride on the #10 bus from Brussels to Sandal Bay as the bus cruised along the open road. Unlike BrownsVille, Sandal Bay sat right on the beach front. The houses in the village decorated the coastline.

Time and time again, the Minister responsible for Community Development cautioned the villagers on the dangers of building their houses so close to the sea; yet, no one listened. Whenever there were high tides and hurricane force winds, the villagers would panic but go right back to fixing the damages incurred through the inclement weather.

Being the contractor that he was, Donté built his house in a through road away from the coastline. His house, built on a small incline, faced the beautiful waters of the bay. Behind his home were many fruit trees the children in the community would raid ever so often. Because of the position of his home, Donté was always safe when natural disasters struck Sandal Bay.

Petra and Cherry practiced what they would say to James when they saw him and what he might have said to them. Petra was more reluctant than Cherry because she had been rude to her father, oftentimes avoiding him when she figured he would come to visit. She didn't understand the reason he left, and it hurt her more than for years, she had clung to the memory of the man she loved the most.

The girls walked up to the veranda and up to the door.
Knock. Knock. Knock.
No one answered.

"Maybe if we bawl dem out, dey go hear?" Cherry suggested.
"Uncle Donté is me. Is Cherry."
No answer.

Petra thought it to be a sign. Maybe it was the perfect time to escape. Maybe they should not have come. Maybe they should have just left the situation alone and let her mother deal with everything that was happening, as the mature adult she was. After all, she always knew best.

Petra had battled many thoughts about her father opening the door: what if he was so hurt by her turning him down that he decided that he didn't want anything to do with her again?

A few seconds after, the door knob turned and a sleepy, familiar face looked through the door. A look of surprise hit both Petra and the man at the door while Cherry smiled for him.

"Hi daddy."

"Gyuls. What allu doin' here?" James asked, "somet'ing happen?"

"No." Cherry responded, looking at Petra to explain to their father that they just wanted to talk. More so Petra, because Cherry had spoken to him a few times since his return.

"We want to talk." Petra finally responded.
"Aa, we?" Cherry interjected. "We is pig language!"

Petra glared at Cherry and would growl at her if she could.
"Ah..." Petra started, "Ah wanted to talk to you an' see how you doin'."

James smiled. He was ecstatic, but he couldn't let his girls see him act like a child in a candy store. He had anticipated this moment for many years, and here they were, reaching out to him. When he thought about the courage Petra must have summed up to be at Donté's front door reaching out to him, he almost shed a tear. But no, he wouldn't seem *less-of-a-man* in front two of the three ladies he loved the most.

"Ah dey." James finally responded. "Ah jus' sit down on de inside watchin' some football dey."
"Wey uncle Donté?" Cherry interjected.
"He doh come yet." Her father responded. "Allu good?"
"Yea, we dey. Wa you do today?" Cherry interjected again.

This time, Petra gave her the look of *you sayin' we is pig language but you cyah seem to hush you mout', na?* Cherry rolled her eyes at Petra and stepped back to sit on the veranda. James understood the non-verbal exchange between his daughters and laughed to himself. Petra had really captured the dominant personality of her mother.

"Cherry, you could go inside an' watch TV if you want."

James didn't have to say much. Cherry sprinted through Uncle Donté's front door and sat on the couch, changing the channel from ESPN to A&E. *Criminal Minds* was currently showing. James looked at Cherry, shook his head and chuckled. He brought his attention back to Petra whose gaze was firm on him. They looked at each other and occasionally looked away. The silence grew between them like a fungus. Eventually, James broke it.

"So what de gyal say?"

Petra sighed, "ah dey. But ah jus' want to know wa happen. How after all dis time, you jus' come back. Uncle Donté always home since we small, he always around bringin' food or money but never once he say anything about you. Why you leave us like da?"

James took a deep breath in and sighed thereafter. "Is a lot ah t'ings, Petty. It have some t'ing ah wish ah could tell you but it so sensitive, ah want to talk to your mother about before ah tell you."

"Mister, ah turnin' twenty-two in March, ah find de time for dis t'ing about you have to talk to mammy first have to stop. Ah lot ah t'ings happen an' ah find is only right we know. We could pretend all we want but everybody know t'ings coulda never be the same when you pack an' go. You come back an' up to now we en know wa happen." James could sense Petra's frustration, but he knew he had to do the right thing.

"Ah want to respect you mudda. You for yourself know how Janice could be. The truth is you similar to her and ah know you want to know but let's be fair."

"Fair?" Petra snarled. "So is fair to tell mammy but not fair for us to know wey you was an' wa you was doin'? Okay. Is ah mistake ah make comin' here!"

James' face filled with sadness. He knew if he didn't say the right thing, the situation would escalate more than it was already blazing out of control. He wanted to talk to the girls in the presence of their mother. The truth was, he didn't feel much of a father after missing out on such a large chunk of their lives.

But he couldn't tell them that. He couldn't bring himself to be so vulnerable in front of his children. It was bad enough he was sitting at the brink of tears and trying to stay strong, but to feel hurt and broken all at the same time, was too overwhelming.

"Petty," James began. "Ah doh want you to ever feel like ah doh want to share t'ings wit' you. Ah jus doh want to upset you mudda. Ah prefer to sit down with all of allu and explain me self. Whether or not allu might believe me, is okay. Ah jus' want to tell the truth about wa I go through an' see how bes' we could move on. An' movin' on could be wit'out me, buh is okay; as long as trut' is trut'."

Petra looked at her father then looked away. She knew he was right. Not only could she read it on his face, she could sense it in the way his voice rattled. *Aww. He want to cry.* She thought to herself.

"Okay. Ah go wait." She finally responded. "So when you comin' over?"

"Ah doh know yet." James responded. "Ah tryin' to see if ah could get allu uncle to talk to you mudda because she doh want me around too much ah hear."

James hung his head in sorrow, looking down on his size 14 feet on the brown tiles. His toes spread flat on the surface, except for his one left pink toe that curled up under his foot. James remembered the days Janice used to laugh at his toe, calling him *curly*. He hated the name and he hated his toe. Every time he looked at his feet, he would remember Janice and the thought of it made him hate himself for the entire situation.

Petra turned around, giving her back completely to James. She wiped the tears that seemed to be rushing down to her blouse. She would never let her father see her crying. She wouldn't even pull up her nose to retract the mucus dripping at the back of her throat and also coming through her nose. Petra held her hand up to her face and pretended to sneeze, releasing the mucus and tears. *She was clever.*

"Ah could get piece ah tissue please?"
"Wa do you?" James asked before stepping into the living room and grabbing the roll on the table. "You ha' de cold?"
"No, me sinus." Petra lied. "Somet'ing maybe raise it."

"Look." James said as he handed her the tissue. "You mus' use wild onion. When allu was small, ah use to give allu dat, especially Cherry. She nose always use to be runnin'"

Cherry walked up to the door, "ah hear me name. Wa allu sayin' about me dey?"

James laughed. "Dat little girl nose use to run bad. Ah remember when you d' start preschool, me and Janice use to have to pin ah washrag with a big diaper pin on you' clothes so you doh lose it."

The three laughed heartily together. Cherry and Petra had remembered the days their mother told them stories of Cherry and her chronic sinusitis, many of which were sad stories of near-death experiences Cherry had as a child. Janice's only option when her three year old would stop breathing at night, was to suck the mucus out of Cherry's nose using her mouth.

Janice used to always tell Cherry *Papa God know why he put you here. So doh play the fool an' let him have to yank you out because of no foolish behaviour eh girl.*

"Wa it was like on the island, daddy?" Cherry asked.

For a second, James had forgotten all of his troubles but the question pulled him back into reality. "It was nice in de beginnin'." He responded. "De place remind me of some parts in Grenada. It had a lot ah rivers an' de beaches was crystal clear waters jus' like how Coastguard beach on the western side is. Waternut trees dey everywhere an' de island was smaller dan Grenada so you could walk 'round it easy. Maybe about twenty-five square miles alone." James paused, "But you see de latter part of de time dey? E' was sour."

Before James could continue, Donté could be seen walking into the gap. Petra looked at the time and the two decided it was time to return home. As they walked from the gap to the bus stop, they greeted Donté as he walked towards his house.

Cherry glanced over at her sister, whose eyes were red and puffy. It was not sinusitis; she could tell Petra had been crying. Cherry felt over the years, she began to understand her sister. She felt like since James' return, Petra was avoiding him. Now, here she was, putting her pride aside and making the effort to see him.

She finally understood that deep without her tough exterior, Petra craved the love and attention her father wanted to give her. He had all the answers to the questions she had.

8 De Trut' is de Trut'

"Dat was the best you could'a come up with, James?" Janice laughed. "You leave us for how much years, an' de bes' you could come up wit' is dat *donkey pee on you* in San Souci? Wi, papa!"

Petra, JJ and Cherry all sat there in silence. It had not sunk into their thoughts completely what their father had explained. When Petra was younger, her father used to read her stories of jumbies as they would call them. They were the Caribbean folklores and tales that flooded the isles during the time of slavery.

A great deal of Grenadians believed that these were made up, while others believed that they were a direct link to many of the Obeah or voodoo practices brought from Africa by the slaves. Whatever their definite origin, the fact remained that many accounted for personal experiences with a number of these creatures.

Many young men in Grenada frequently told tales of La Diablesse making sexual advances to them and having to flee for their lives. Others, such as fishermen, told tales of mermaids calling out to them early mornings, while they were on sea to join them in the water for sexual pleasure.

There was the La Diablesse, Mama Malade, Soucouyant and her male counterpart, the Lougarou. Whatever the *jumbie*, every islander in Grenada and the Grenadine Isles had a story. As for James, his encounter with the La Diablesse and him being trapped on San Souci by Obeah was one he had tried his best to keep to himself.

But now, he realised how trapped he continued to feel going through this ordeal alone. His desire to share with the people closest to him, the ones he thought he had hurt, felt like the right thing to do but it was not well received by Janice.

Janice stood up and took two steps away from James. She was beginning to lose her temper, but today, she decided she would think through her words and visualise them before she spoke to her estranged husband.

"James, if you know what good for you, you go come out in me face with that schupidness, one time!"

"Janice," James started, "Ah doh come to fight. You know how hard it was for me to relive dis t'ing for a second time? Ah had to sit down an' tell Donté, after all the years ah never could'a bring me-self to tell him de trut'. You really feel ah go sit down here, an' lie for you when all ah really want is..." James stopped.

Janice's facial expression did not denote one of pleasure, but one of annoyance and frustration. She did not understand how he would even think about telling her that all he wanted was to get his family back together and make up for lost times.

James looked down at the carpet under his feet and thought about the times he and Janice playfully fought on evenings. The love he shared for her was real. He could blame his desire to make money, his lack of a grounded spiritual life or be spiteful towards the *demons* responsible for where his life was now, but nothing could change what happened, or make up for the time he lost.

"Ah doh askin' for much; ah jus' need you to hear me out. Listen to me." James begged, but when he sensed her reluctance, he couldn't fight any longer.

"Alright Janice," he finally said. "If you en wan' to hear the trut' from me, at least hear Donté out. Maybe you might listen to him instead."

James' estranged wife was silent – from anger or just speechless from what he said but James couldn't decipher, so he called Donté, who was sitting on the veranda while the children went to their bedrooms.

Donté walked into the quiet house and glanced around. It had been quite some time since he stepped foot into his cousin's home, many years for that matter. He remembered when he and James built the three-bedroom structure, the many days of fun and laughter. At that time, Donté and Janice were already great friends.

People always wondered how James was so comfortable with his *womanising* cousin being so close to his wife. And of course, Ms. Millie had already speculated that *donkey was in*

James cane. But the relationship the trio had before the children were born was unbreakable. Their bond was inseparable. That was until James went away for eight years and never returned up until now. It had been about three months since James came back to Grenada, but nothing seemed to have changed, except for his new relationship with his children.

~

Donté walked into the dining room where Janice and James were quietly seated. The air in the room was so tense, still and cold that Donté wanted to leave, but he knew he had to help his cousin make it right, even if he didn't understand how he could do so.

"What sense you could make outta dis nonsense this good-for-not'ing man comin' an' tell me here now, Donté?"

What a way to start. He thought to himself. "Believe me Janice," Donté started, "Ah was jus' as shock' as you when he tell me dis t'ing, but you know dem stories about de crazy t'ings dat does happen in San Souci."

"An' you believe him?" Janice asked hastily, "you foolish enough to believe him, an' you want me look like a fool too? Dat is wha' you come here for? To back up you cousin an' make me look schupid?"

Donté refused to answer. He knew how easy it was for Janice to lose her temper and blow the smallest of things out of proportion. That in itself seemed to aggravate Janice even more.

"So you go jus' stand up dey an' doh say not'ing?"

James looked over at Donté, and Donté could see the frustration in his eyes. It didn't take long for James to lose him temper, "You wanted de trut', ah give it to you. If ah was really doin' wha' dey tell you ah was doing, ah would'a understand. Ah put me-self outta me way to make me-self look less dan a man in front of you. All dis insults an' all dis t'ings you tell me really hurtin' me, an' ah fed up! Ah tryin' me best. You doh want me, look me chil'ren and dem doh even know me much less to want me. You fin' da easy to deal with? Eh? Answer me dat! Look, ah try me bes' but if you doh wan' to believe me, ah cyah force you. Ah go leave you alone, ah go move on, ah sorry ah even try to come an' be hones' wit' you, Janice."

James got up off the chair and jerked it under the table in haste. He stormed through the kitchen and went down the back step. He walked down to the ravine, close to Mr. Joe's house and sat on the big stone, his back turned to Mr. Joe's residence. His reflection in the water was clear, even with the tears streaming down his face. His sobs were silent, but his pain was loud. It had been so long since he had felt this broken, especially by the woman he loved.

But could he blame her? Janice had a right to feel that way. She wasn't there with him in his travails in San Souci and if he were her, he wouldn't believe his story either. Even as a believer in God and a man who grew up hearing about those

Caribbean tales of *La Diablesse* and the like, James never thought in all of his life, that experience would be as real as it was for him. At times, he wished he didn't remember. The nightmares were still real, and the constant reminder of Pastor Branson in San Souci to keep praying and studying the Word was feeling too overwhelming for him.

He could never forget the moment he was broken from the chains that had him bound. The three-night prayer and fast, the demons around him that told him he was going to die, the angel he was so sure he saw covering him with a white cloak and the sound of wailing and screeching that almost busted his ear drums.

James taught about the years of bondage that seemed to become normalised. But who was Janice to believe him? She wasn't there, she didn't feel what he felt or the times when he tried to call her but he couldn't, unable to make decisions on his own.

James wondered to himself what he would tell his children. Petra, who was already in her twenties, would never believe that her father was trapped by the creatures in stories he told her as a child. Cherry, as sweet as she was, she might still be sceptical just as her mother about James' return. Although he had developed a bond with James Jr, how long would it last now that JJ heard his truth? Would it have been worth it?

~

As James sat contemplating his existence and the pain his own mishap brought to his family, he heard the familiar sound of whistling. James smiled. It had been many years since he heard that distinct whistle and more so, that exact tune. He quickly wiped the tears from his face before he lifted his head in the direction of the sound. He supposedly lifted his head too quick before the whistler was nowhere to be found.

"Ah tell you I'm ah hard man to ketch." The whistler shouted from the distance. "You does hear dem comin' but dey does cyan see you."

James laughed and his laugh was echoed by Mr. Joe's distinct laughter. James had not seen Mr. Joe in years but his voice sounded the same. As he walked through the bushes not far from the bank, James' eyebrows lifted in awe. He looked the same. No one could tell how old he was and he would tell no one either, but whatever he was doing and whatever he was eating, James wanted a part in it too.

"Joe," James laughed, "Man, you doh changin'! You doh even look like you age."
Joe laughed heartily, "Ah one cent cyan change, Jamesy."
The two men laughed together.
"Wa de man say?" Joe asked as he looked in James' direction.
"Ah dey." James lied.
"You know you didn' have to wipe de tears eh." Joe said, "Man is man, an' de kinda feelin's you mus'e have inside you now wit' everyt'ing da goin' on, is okay to cry sometimes."

James sighed. He didn't have to be reassured, but somehow, it felt good to feel Joe noticed and his care and compassion was there, even in his old age.

"Ah had a feelin' you went through a bit of what ah went through when ah went to San Souci." Joe stated as he turned to James."

"Donté tell you?" James asked hesitantly. He was already embarrassed by the situation, and now he couldn't believe his cousin was telling everyone his business.

"Donté en tell me not'ing sunny boy. Ah could'a tell was somet'ing like wa happen to me across dey dat happen to you. Ah good man like you James, would neva go an' jus' leave Janice an' dem chil'ren like dat."

Before Mr. Joe could finish, James interrupted. "wa you mean de same t'ing happen to you?"
"Jus' like ah tell you, James."

James' heart sank into the big stone he was sitting on. Since his return, he had felt nothing but ridicule and shame. He was now a broken man fighting to defend his honour with truths so bare and naked. Yet, no one believed him. The two people he counted on the most couldn't fathom this *truth* and although Donté was finding his way to accept that maybe, in fact, this had happened to his cousin, there were still doubts in his mind.

Janice, on the other hand, had not given it a chance to soak in that maybe James was telling the truth. But her stubbornness wouldn't allow her to see past the hurt and hear him out. Then there were his children, caught in the middle of their own perception and feelings: an estranged father long gone, now returning and expecting a relationship from them.

James himself knew exactly how they felt, and it bothered him that he was not there for them but especially his son, JJ. After the death of his twin brother Eric, James' father Erol did not recover from his grief. His frustration and brokenness drove a wedge between him and his wife.

Erol left the home when James was 17, leaving his mother alone to raise him, the only son. His mother grew him up strict, teaching him the ways of being a man but respecting women. Janice always admired that about him, his love for his family and the values that he had.

But now, James could only imagine Janice, being the woman that she was to feel hurt immensely, viewing him as nothing, but a liar and a cheater. He wanted to understand how she felt but his feelings of hurt rose within him. He thought about the many times he forgave her and the countless hours they spent hashing out unresolved issues because he loved her so much. Now, when it came to him, she couldn't believe him.

Yet, Mr. Joe, a man of mystery, who was standing over him as he looked at his pitied reflection in the water, was telling him he understood his treacherous experience first-hand? James felt a feeling of hope as he looked up at the old man.

"Wa de happen, Joe?" James asked.
"Come," Joe responded, "take a walk wit' me to de ol' house lemme tell you wa happen. Ah keep ah lot ah secrets in me life ahready, ah lot ah dem was worth keepin', ah lot ah dem

wasn' wort' it ah-tall, but ah believe ah go through dis one so ah could help you in some way."

James got up from the rock and followed Mr. Joe as they walked to his small concrete structure. As the men talked on their way to the house, James felt a bit lighter, he felt that maybe even if he could not get his family back, he would lay his experience to rest.

9 La-Jah-Bless

James was astounded. A man of many secrets like Mr. Joe had gone through such a turmoil, even worse than James did, and he was able to survive and tell his story. James sat on the wooden arm chair in quiet as Mr. Joe rocked slowly in his old rocking chair and intently looked at James.

"You see dis t'ing call prayer? You cyah go wrong dey, Jamesy." Mr. Joe sat up in his rocking chair, his feet halting the motion instantly. "Even if you en believe in the big man upstairs, you always have dis little bit ah faith inside you da does nudge you to want to reach out to *somet'ing* greater than you."

James understood Mr. Joe all too well. Not everything around him was all trouble once in his life. In fact, he used to be a sold-out Christian man before life began moving before his eyes. As Mr. Joe spoke, James remembered the days he spent at his Christian college fellowshipping and engaging in worship with his brothers and sisters in Christ. Oftentimes, his lecturer, Mr. Ramsey warned James and his companions about starting off so hot.

He would say, "You only have once to be a man, all the other times, you will do childish things. Be wise, and make wiser decisions. This Christian walk is no joke. You start out hot today and by tomorrow, if you aren't grounded, you will be cold."

As Mr. Joe spoke about his personal experience, James felt he was right. For many years he looked at his wife Janice being the home-maker, the prayer-warrior, the glue that held their union together, and an overall power house. He loved her more than she could have possibly fathomed, but James knew, at times his *love* was not enough.

Janice wanted a man who would pray and not worry, a man who she could pray with and who would cover her. James knew, in that area, he had failed her miserably. Many times, he felt football was more important than prayer meetings, that crayfish hunting meant more than prayer and fast or family devotions and that Sunday was sufficient to give praises to God.

Janice and James argued many times about the way the girls would be raised. Janice thought that her children would grow up in the fear of the Lord, while James thought it best that the decision would be theirs when or if they chose to serve God. For Janice, Christianity meant everything; she was raised in a God-fearing home by parents who were ministers.

Janice was taught that God had to be served as human beings were created to serve and worship Him. Janice never strayed from that. Similarly, James grew up in a home with a mother who was a bible-believer. However, because of the many rules James had to live by, he always felt that his children would not be forced into believing and growing up in a religion they didn't feel comfortable in.

As time went by, Janice continued to pray that James would find his way, asking God to teach him a lesson when James' choices seemed too ridiculous to accept.

As Mr. Joe continued to talk to James about his personal experience and admonished James on bringing this challenge to God in prayer, James thought to himself, *"Maybe this was why it was so easy for me to be trapped and bounded by these chains."*

~

"Mammy, ah know you might tell me dat is not we place, but all of us ah part of this t'ing too. Ah find we should hear him out." Petra looked at her mother's bloodshot eyes, wild with anger and did not look away.

It had been a while since she stood up to her mother in the midst of conflicting ideas. Often times, Petra second-guessed herself when it came to disagreeing with her mother; Janice frequently made the children feel like their opinion didn't matter.

When Janice and Miss Millie were on speaking terms, Miss Millie used to say, "Janice, you go push you chil'ren away." But Janice never listen to Miss Millie. Who would have? Miss Millie's bad reputation always was before her as her intentions were never pure.

"For what? Janice responded. "You believe dat foolishness allu fadda say dey?"

"Is not about believe or not mammy," Petra continued. "is about givin' de man he chance to explain he-self."

Janice sucked her teeth but Petra paid her no mind. "You know how much times, as ah child, ah sit down here waitin' for him to come home? Or how much times ah sit down in me room an' hear you cry when…"

Before Petra could finish, Janice interrupted, "an' wa da ha to do wit' any'ting chil'?"

"Everyt'ing!" Petra exclaimed. "Everyt'ing! We hurting jus' how you hurtin' too! Me an' Cherry only had ah little time to have a relationship wit' de man, but what about JJ? So we doh deserve ah chance to understand his side ah de story too?"

Janice grew frustrated, "likkle gyul, you better watch you tone wit' me eh!"

Petra sighed, "Mammy, ah sorry, but you not de only one here dat affected. Think about us too. We have a right to understand wa happen an' how bes' we could move forward. Whether movin' forward is wit' him or wit'out him, we have ah right to try."

Janice knew that even if she never admitted it, Petra was right. James missed out on a great part of the children's life and it had affected them all. She couldn't spend the rest of her life being angry at the man she knew she still loved and was still in love with her. She understood that it would take time, but she had to give him the chance to make it right, at least for his three children.

"He go ahready?" Janice finally asked the children.

"JJ say he see him over by Mr. Joe talkin'." Cherry responded.
"Go an' call him?" JJ inquired.

Janice knew she wanted to say yes but she didn't want the
children to feel like they were her mediator between her and
their father. Whatever differences they had, they would sort
it out as parents and as adults.

"Is alright JJ," she finally responded. "Ah go talk to him
later."

The children got up from around the dining table and
journeyed to the living room, leaving Janice alone lost in her
thoughts. Not much was said, but a lot could be sensed
though they were silent.

Not long after, JJ turned to his sisters and asked, "allu find
dat jumbie story is real?"
Cherry sat up in the chair and looked at Petra, then JJ and
said, "Ah en know. Wa allu find?"
Petra sighed, "ah doh believe he come back here after all dis
time to lie for us, an' Uncle Donté de look convinced in
trut'."

"You ever see ah jumbie?" JJ asked his sisters.

Petra looked at JJ and shrugged her shoulders, "Ah hear
mammy say it had ah time she hear cousin Michelle say she
catch Peter down de road in she house countin' salt.
Remember dey say dey could use dat to catch dem Lougarou
an' Soucouyant an' dem."

"Wa you find, Cherry?" JJ asked intently as he stared at his older sister.

"Ah find is true." Cherry responded. "Ah tell allu ahready ah see ball ah fire shootin' across de sky. It have real jumbie on dis island. Ah sure all dem island an' dem in de Grenadine Isles an' maybe even de Caribbean too have somet'ing."

~

The children continued their chatter sharing tales of the times they heard people in the village or on other parts of the island sharing stories of the creatures they had encountered. Of the many stories they shared, Cherry remembered the moment Danisha shared with her an experience her father had:

It was a moonlight night in Soleil Rouge sometime in the seventies. Twenty-year-old Dominic had just left his twenty-year-old girlfriend, Marisha's house. Marisha lived in Soleil Rouge at the west end of the island and Dominic lived in L'ance Aux Serpents, at the south east end of the island, about thirty minutes walking distance.

Mr. Dominic had just gotten his license but he did not own a car so he would walk to and from Marisha's house. The pair had been dating for over a year and Dominic had promised to propose to Marisha as soon as he had accumulated enough money.

On the night in question, Dominic left Soleil Rouge around half past nine and was journeying back to his home. It was not unusual for him to walk alone; in fact, it was at those moments he spent time thinking about the love of his life, Marisha.

About half way through his journey, Dominic heard what sounded like shoe heels clicking behind him and the sweet hum of a song he did not know. The sound was hard to miss. As he turned around, he noticed a young woman walking behind him. He had never seen her before and was unable to catch a glimpse of her face.

"Quite ah night for ah young lady like you-self to be walkin' alone." He said but she did not respond. "Wey you from?" No response.

Dominic figured that the young lady might have been afraid that the man ahead of her could have attacked her, so he left her alone. Again, Dominic looked back to see more of the young woman's attire and physique being defined in the moonlight. He continued on his way and tried not to bother her.

If Marisha was on the road alone and a young man was walking ahead of her, he too would not have expected her to start a conversation with him. God forbid!

Dominic continued walking and for the last time, he felt compelled to ask the young woman if she was lost and needed help. He looked back to see her long black hair bouncing on the shoulders of her white dress that hugged her well-defined body.

Although he was dating Marisha, he could not help but notice how good her silhouette looked.

As the moon shone in the sky, he looked in her direction and asked, "Miss, you sure you doh need no help?"

No response.

He looked ahead and again turned around. It was almost like a compulsion. This time, she walked directly under the old street light before the Saint Martin village and the unthinkable was revealed! The woman wore a big brown straw hat that covered her face but revealed her jet-black hair falling off her shoulders and unto her white dress that flowed to the ground, hiding what could have been kitten heels. *Clop. Clop. Clop.*

It did not take Dominic long to realise that the woman behind him was not lost, but pursuing him in an effort to trap him, seduce him and take his soul. Fear gripped Dominic and he began to run, yelling as loudly as he could, "La Diablesse! La Diablesse!"

The pace of what previously sounded like heels began to increase just as quickly as Dominic sprinted away from the jumbie. He knew there and then, it was not shoe heels but one cow hoof accompanied by a human foot.

"La Diablesse! La Diablesse!" Dominic continued to scream at the top of his lungs.

In less than a few minutes, the lights in the houses just a few meters away from him were turned on and people came out into the streets. Just as would be expected, the jumbie, not interested in a crowd but in the man ahead of her, disappeared into the moonlight night, leaving Dominic panting uncontrollably and very much afraid.

The villagers ran towards him with many questions and concerns. They gave him a glass of water and wanted to send him on his way. Yet, Dominic insisted that he was not going to walk the rest of the way alone. A welcoming family let him spend the rest of the night in their spare room until morning had dawned. Dominic was sure that if he had turned around to assist her, she would have seduced him and put him in a trance where he would have walked to the river bank and drowned.

~

Janice looked at the phone in her hand and for the third time, she put it down on the table, before picking it up again a few seconds later. She sucked her teeth. She wondered when she would sum up the courage to put her anger aside and just call Donté to ask about James' whereabouts. After their supposed family meeting turned sour, Janice had not spoken to Donté or to her estranged husband, James.

Janice had battled in her mind the necessity of making amends for the sake of their family union but nothing seemed definite to her. She was too afraid of the hurt and pain that would be inflicted on her and her children again if James were to leave another time. She had spent most of the day on work daydreaming and lost in her own thoughts about the madness that had been revealed to her.

Of the many stories she had heard and the opinions of those around her, her husband was back with a tale of being trapped on the neighbouring island of San Souci by a La Diablesse while working on a Soucouyant's house. But when the idea seemed too preposterous in her mind, Janice would suck her teeth and ask herself, "so James feel ah schupid or wa?"

It was a quarter to five and the children were out in the road playing, while Petra sat on the step talking to her co-worker Json making *Carriacou love*. Janice sighed, and for the final time, she picked up the landline and dialled Donté's number.

One ring. Two rings. Three rings. Four...

"Hello?" the husky voice on the other end said.
Janice froze. It was James.
"Hello??" he said again.
"Afternoon, James." Janice muttered as her voice trembled on the other end.
"Janice?" James asked. Indeed, he was shocked that she was calling Donté's residence.
"Yes is me." She responded.
"If you lookin' for Donté, he step out de road to come back." James said.

Janice sighed. She felt his reluctance to talk to her and she was a little upset that he would suggest she was calling to speak to Donté. James knew all too well that Janice was reaching out to him, but like the typical island man, he was playing *hard-to-get*.

127

"Ah doh call to talk to Donté, ah call to talk to you." Janice finally responded.

"Hmm." James scoffed under his breath. "What for? Ent you make it clear you doh want to have not'ing to do wit' me?"
Janice held back her desire to tell James off and said, "look, ah doh call you to argue. Ah call you to ask if we could try again. For de sake ah de chil'ren, leh we see if we could sit down another time an' make sense of dis nonsense. Dem chil'ren miss out on too much of you in dey life ahready for you to have to come back an' t'ings doh workin' ahready."

"Hmm, ah go t'ink about it." James said, and before Janice had a chance to respond James said he had to go and handle some business, and hung up the phone.

Janice sat alone in the house battling the thoughts that raced through her mind. She was angry at herself for seeming so vulnerable by reaching out to James and she was angry with him for how rude he was. But could she blame him? The way in which she treated him was uncalled for. Yes, she had a right to be upset and taken aback by what he had revealed but the man needed a break, *didn't he?*

~

"You could believe she call here today an' askin' me to come back to do de same t'ing ah try to do de las' time ah was dey? Boy woman hard to please!"

Donté could sense James' frustration and before long, James had begun pacing back and forth in the living room. It was something he did when he was nervous, angry or anticipating a favourable outcome.

In the moment, his pacing was a combination of all three feelings and he knew even though he made Janice feel that he would think about it, he didn't need to. He knew that putting aside his feelings for the sake of his children was more important to him than whatever disagreements he and Janice had.

He understood quite clearly the need for him to make up for the time he had lost enduring his spiritual ordeal in San Souci. Yet, most of all, James knew that deep within him was a desire to hold the woman he loved once more in his arms, embracing her closely, telling her how sorry he was for being such a fool and letting the unthinkable happen.

"Sit down na boy!" Donté shouted at James. "You only pacin' an' it makin' me nervous!"

Immediately, James took a seat. He picked up the cold Mackeson he had opened a while earlier and took a mouthful.

He sighed. "Ah part ah me want to forget her an' jus' mind me chil'ren but ah know dat wouldn' make no sense. You could believe Janice, boy?"

Donté knew no words he spoke could have cheered his cousin up but he tried to be as optimistic as he could. "She jus' need some time to cool down, an' it could be time she get to t'ink about wa you say so she makin' de effort. Ah know Janice head hard as much as she hard to please but one en different dan de other. Two of allu is de same t'ing an' we know if somebody doh compromise, dis go drag on for years. Be de bigger person an' show Janice de man she know you could be. You know is you alone da could get her out of she funk."

James knew Donté was right so he picked up the phone and dialled Janice's number. He hoped for the best but still expected the worse because anything could happen when Janice was upset.

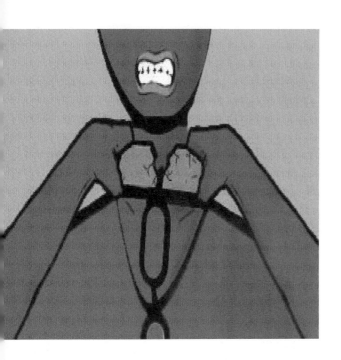

131

10 Enough is Enough

"You find mammy go make him move back in with us?" Cherry asked Petra, who was sitting on the step just below her.

"Ah doh know." Petra responded.

"Well," Cherry continued. "Ah like when he does come around. It does be like he de never go in the firs' place."

Petra smiled. She may not have wanted to admit that having her father around the past few months was a fulfilling experience, but the truth remained that James' return and Janice's effort to make the unpleasant situation work, was worth it.

A lot had changed since James' came back to Grenada. San Souci was a terrible experience for him and he did not want to relive it.

James and Janice had decided to compromise and go to counselling. The entire situation was not easy for Janice. Her pride would not allow her let go of the moments when she felt James had abandoned her and the children. Yet the more she hated him, the more she loved him. The more she resented what occurred in the past, the more she wanted to understand his emotions: how he felt, how much he would have needed her, how much he felt alone. She loved him;

that was something she had to admit, even when she thought she couldn't.

Every Tuesday morning, James and Janice would go to Pastor Samuel's deliverance sessions. After the counselling started a few months ago, the minister revealed that there were spiritual forces still at work in James' lives. This was evident in James' inability to sleep at nights and reoccurring dreams of being fed in his sleep.

In African and Grenadian dream interpretations, eating or being fed in a dream meant that someone was trying to tie that individual in the spiritual world. By doing so, that person could manipulate and control the actions and moods of the other person. Janice knew her vow for *for better or worse* meant she had to support James spiritually. She would get up early in the morning and go down on her knees on his behalf.

Her decision to put the past behind occurred when she had a dream that confirmed that in fact, James had been tied in the spirit world, but it was never revealed by who. No amount of anger or hatred could help her and her family, so she decided to let bygones be bygones and be the support her husband needed.

Many of the deliverance sessions continued to expose areas in the Hopkins' lives and the family that needed to be mended and doors that needed to be closed in order for complete healing to take place. It seemed odd to the children to have to spend mornings praying for hours but Janice insisted that in order to get through as a family, they had to work together as the unit they were.

Since James returned, a lot changed in Petra's life. She began dating Json who was more than a support to her. She never imagined that she would find someone who understood her personality, yet tried to look past her flaws and see the real person she was on the inside. Petra had dated boys in high school but nothing was serious until Json.

He too had spent nights with the family being a source of encouragement to Petra and her mother when things seemed overwhelming. At first, James did not approve of Petra having a boyfriend, but eventually, remembered that she wasn't the thirteen-year-old he left and that she had blossomed into a beautiful woman.

James and JJ's bond continued to flourish. JJ spent days at Donté's house with his father bonding over fishing, crayfish trapping and their all-time-favourite, football.

"You have a girlfrien'?" James would ask his young son, but JJ would only laugh and shy away from the question.

"When I was ah little boy like you," James started, "ah used to t'ink marriage an' relationship wasn' for me. Ask you uncle, all de girls used to be by we. But dat is not wat life is about me boy. You ha' to study you head, get you education an' find ah nice woman, one like you mudda, an' settle down wit' her."

"So you comin' back home?" JJ asked, straying away from the discussion his father started knowing well that James was right.

"Dat is up to you' mudda, wi." James responded. "Ah doh tryin' to rush ha into anyt'ing."

No amount of time and effort could make up for what was lost but the family could have done everything in their power to turn over a new leaf and write a new page. With all his anticipation, James knew he had to be patient with Janice. He knew if he rushed too soon, things would not move smoothly. He wanted things to happen at the right time.

That afternoon, James decided he would pay Janice a visit, bringing her a pot of turkey soup – just the way she liked it. As he walked towards the house, he looked over to Miss Millie's house, only to see her peering through her curtain. He said no words to her and moved quickly before she approached him. James walked up the street to the house and knocked on the door. He took off his slipper and entered when Janice answered.

"Afternoon everybody." James said as he walked towards the kitchen, leaving the container he had prepared earlier on the counter.
"Afternoon." Janice answered. "What you bring dey?"
"Turkey soup," he said. "Jus' the way you like it."

Janice smiled. If it was one person in the world, other than her late mother, who would understand her love for turkey soup, it was James. She leaned over his shoulder and hugged him. James was flushed but he could not pretend. He was happy indeed that the ordeal was coming to an end.

Later on in the evening, after having lunch together, the children all went their separate ways, leaving their parents to talk. Petra hugged her father and went into her room to call Json, Cherry kissed James on the cheek and entered her room to begin reading *The Venus Conspiracy*, and JJ gave James a bounce as he left for football practice. The children left Janice and James in the dining room talking, deciding how they would move forward.

It had almost been a year since James' return and the process seemed long, hard and slow but it was worth it. The effort, the patience, the moments were all worth it in the end. James knew that he would never trade the opportunity he had to reconnect and reconcile with the people he loved the most.

Not long after, Janice and James walked to the veranda to have a more private discussion. Janice knew that the girls were excited about their father moving back home and the walls had ears. So, to avoid any premature ideas, Janice asked James to sit in the hammock with her so they could talk.

"Jus' like ol' times, eh?" James said as he looked into Janice's eyes, glancing at how full her cheeks had become.
"Jus' like ol' time for real. You remember when we use' to rock here an' fall asleep?" she asked.
"How ah go forget dat, girl?" said James.

~

Just as it was expected, it didn't take long for Ms. Millie to show up to start to mind Janice's business again. It could never be understood how that woman was so inquisitive; she didn't want Janice's friendship, yet, she spent most of her time focused and fixated on Janice's life.

Cherry was lying on her bed reading when she heard, "James-o! Is you dat dey, boy?" It was Miss Millie.

Cherry got off her bed as quickly as Speedy Gonzales moved, not in an effort to put her mouth where it didn't belong but to calm her mother down. Cherry knew Janice was very close to losing her temper with Miss Millie. Janice had spent a lot of time, the night before, complaining about Miss Millie's lies and the deceptive nature she portrayed to the people around her.

A few of the villagers expressed to Janice the negative ideas Miss Millie attempted to put in their heads when James returned, all of which were lies. Janice referred to her as the pompous neighbourhood CCTV camera.

As the chattering continued outside, Cherry stood by the door peering through the louvers, Petra called out to her "Cherry, doh bother go outside dey eh; all dah goin' an happen dey goin' an happen for a reason. Jus' let it be girl."

"But Petra," Cherry responded. "mammy go put down she Christianity cloak for dat woman called Miss Millie. Ah cyah si'dung   so   an   watch   her   do   dat."
"Gyul," Petra insisted, "ah tell you to leave it alone. If mammy doh deal with all ah dat years ah pent up frustration now, ah bet you she go regret it in the end. Leave dem people alone leh dey sort out dey business. Whatever she tell Miss Millie, know dat dah woman had it coming to her a long

time   now."

Petra had a point. They could remember the years Janice's pain overlapped into the way she treated her children. The more Miss Millie fed the gossiping community of BrownsVille with news, the more Janice felt hurt and betrayed by someone she once called her friend.

Cherry eventually retreated into her room and listened to the advice of her big sister. She got back into bed and picked up the thriller novel she was reading earlier, trying her best to ignore the commotion she knew was about to unravel.

As she flipped through the pages, she thought about Professor Bacci and this discovery he had that would allow him to control human emotions such as falling in love. At that very moment, Cherry wished she was professor Bacci and that she could inject her parents with the same drug he created that would make her parents put the past behind and inevitably fall in love. Maybe that way, all the pain they both felt would stop and everything would finally get back to normal.

As Cherry wandered in her own thoughts, she was quickly dragged away from the tranquillity when the chatter and small talk was cut by her father. "Now is not a good time to chat, Miss   Millie.   Ah   go   see   you   later."

Miss Millie didn't wait but responded, "Now is not the best time ah know. You come back to make it up to the wifey but leh me see how you lookin' dey na, boy. Look how long ah doh   see   you."

"Ah   little   later   Miss   Millie."   James   insisted.

For a second, Petra, who was listening intently, began to become less anxious when her mother did not respond. Petra knew if Janice had something to say, she would have said it already because she was not afraid of Miss Millie the way some of the other neighbours were afraid of her. Petra started thinking to herself that maybe her mother was at a place where she couldn't care about Miss Millie and her *fass'ness* any longer. Both Petra and Cherry listened closer.

Miss Millie started up again, "Later? So you come back for good James-o? Like you finally come back to you' senses."

Bunjay. Leave it to Miss Millie to ruin a good moment with her pompousness.

"Miss Millie, now is not the best time okay." You could sense James' agitation and frustration in the sound of his voice.

Yet, Miss Millie still kept pushing, "James you en even know if ah go be home later, ah little talk now won' be bad."

The wrath that poured down after that sentence sent an alarm to all the neighbours on Conch Street and the rest of streets in BrownsVille. Petra ran out to the living room. Cherry, who was lying down on her bed, jumped up and rushed out of her room repeating to herself, "ent ah tell Petra da would'a happen!"

Some of the things that left Janice's lips could never be repeated:

"Stinkin' dutty scrutch Millie! You en hear dat man say now is not de time? Like you come across here wit'out you four eyes, an' you cyah see me an' dat man talking? Look! I find is high time you start to take you nose outta people business and focus on yours. From the time dat man leave here, you mindin' me and me chil'ren business. Is like you cyah help it but to be fass? You runnin' you mouth on us from sun up to sun down but yet for all, you never talkin' about *your* business like you does talk about mine. Why you en talk about Winston an' de twelve children he have outside dey with you sister an' two ah de ladies from you Shango Baptist church? Why you en talk about the *fares* you had to make to get the piece ah land next to yours or the Obeah man you went to, to find out wey Winston was the last three years you couldn' see him? Eh Millie? Why you en talk about the fifty pounds you *thief* from Ol' Man Joe the last time you look after he house when he went England, or de fact that you not even sure if Marcus   is   *really*   Winston   own?"

Janice took one slow, long drawn out breath and stared at Miss Millie as Miss Millie just looked at her with utter shock in her eyes and her mouth wide open as if she was catching flies. But it was almost as if that made Janice even more upset.

"Doh watch me so Millie! What you watchin' me so for? Eh? Ah *hold me tongue* for too long! You out there mindin' other people business but you doh want nobody mind yours? Watch! Ah giving you five seconds to come out in me yard before ah start tellin' everybody who come out to mind your business now, all de t'ings you used to sit down an' tell me!"

Before Janice could finish, the streets were filled with people from near and far with their eyes, nose and mouths opened in shock. It had always been said that Janice had a hot mouth but that did not do her fiery personality any justice. A lot of people in the community stated that Janice seemed to calm down since being married to James, but no one really understood how *calm* she really was until then.

Neither Petra, Cherry or JJ had even seen Janice lose her temper as much as she did with Miss Millie that day. It was clear. She had about enough. Janice stood on the veranda staring Miss Millie dead in her eyes, with both her hands dead at her side. Her eyes were wild and her chest heaved uncontrollably. She resembled Mr. Joe's bull again.

What was funnier was the way everyone couldn't help but notice Miss Millie. She quickly retreated to her house with her tail between her fat legs just like a dog admitting defeat. For all the things Janice said to her, she never responded or threatened her. Petra caught a glimpse of her standing there with her eyes wide open before she ran away, and she couldn't help but laugh.

The people in the community were cheering Janice on.
"E' dash good!" Sammy shouted.
"She had it comin', dat wicked woman doh easy, boy." said Ms. Tammy who wore nothing but her towel around her and soap at the back of her neck. You could tell she ran out of

her outside bathroom all the way down Santoepee Street unto Conch Street, when she heard the commotion.

"Yes Janice! Dat good for you, Millie!" Greg laughed as he staggered away from the rum shop. "Stay somethin' now, na?"

James must have known Janice good enough to understand that she needed not to be stopped or told to calm down. Janice needed the moment to release the negativity she had within her for Miss Millie. It was over. She was over Miss Millie and her nonsense. James just stepped back, giving Janice her space. From that day onward, everybody in BrownsVille knew not to mess with Janice.

James looked over at Janice and began to laugh under his breath. Janice looked at him and they both laughed. She smiled. It was the first time in a long time, they were genuine in their feelings and emotions. Janice knew she missed the calmness James brought to her and James missed her smile. They loved each other, and despite their differences and the chains that once had him bound, they vowed that day onward to work on making the family unit and marriage work.

Petra and Cherry looked through the window and smiled at their parents. They had longed for this day to come. Petra, for the answers she sought in her father, Cherry, for the love of her father and the understanding of her mother, and JJ, for the bond with his father. James held Janice in his arms, and for the first time in almost nine years, he reached down and held her chin.

Before he could let his lips meets hers, Cherry whispered, "Oh geed! Dey goin' an' kiss!" Petra shut the blinds as the sisters laughed together. They couldn't wait for JJ to come home to tell him about what transpired.

Epilogue

Miss Millie stood in her dining room looking at Janice as she swayed in her rocking chair. The chair was old; it was Janice's first wedding gift given by her mother. For the last two months, Miss Millie stayed indoors and watched Janice as she spent her early mornings meditating on *God's Word* while the children slept. Miss Millie still felt ashamed and hurt by the verbal assault she received from Janice. She would see James walking down to Conch Street to the residence to look for Janice and the children, and she would see him leave.

Two months had passed and he was still living with Donté. Maybe Janice was not going to take him back. Since the incident with her and Janice, Miss Millie had little to nothing to say to anyone in the community. But as for Janice, she showed no emotions. That made Miss Millie feel horrible, that not once did Janice come over to apologise at least for the embarrassment she put her through.

She hated her. It didn't take long until the last remnants of their understanding dissipated and no words were exchanged between the two. By then, Miss Millie was more than familiar with James and Janice's schedule; it was a quarter to seven in the morning, and by then, James should have been on the way to the house. *Where was he?*

On this Saturday morning, Janice seemed calm and collected, unlike other days when she seemed worried and frustrated. She wore a smile on a face, one which she hadn't in quite some time. Not long after, James walked up to the house and sat in the chair next to Janice. He kissed her on the lips and Miss Millie's stomach flopped. She hated the way things had worked out between them. Oftentimes, their cordial relationship and new understanding made her hate the way she and her common-law husband were presently. She wished to the heavens things between James and Janice were back to the way they were.

Miss Millie sucked her teeth when she heard James and Janice laugh in unison and saw the way James looked at Janice. *Why dat cyah be me?* She secretly thought to herself that if she could only convince Winston to come back home and work things out with her, it would all be alright. But he chose to stay at his own house, doing whatever he wanted, giving other women children when all he gave her was worries and problems.

Miss Millie turned away from the window facing the Hopkins' residence and paced in her living room. In less than two minutes, she peered through the window again. It seemed to her that the relationship between the pair was stronger than before; Janice was very close to letting James move back into the house and they could save their marriage. Miss Millie's desire to be in the know in another person's business seemed to escalate. Had she not learnt her lesson?

Yet another time, Miss Millie walked away from the window and walked towards the small closet space between her kitchen and her storage room. She lifted the lock and pushed the key she wore around her neck into the small hole in the *Master* padlock. When she turned the key, the latch clicked and opened. She removed it from the latch and left it hanging on the hook it was once over. She pulled the wooden door and put her head into the closet in the hopes of finding what she was looking for. Miss Millie reached in and pulled out a shoe box that was lodged under several other boxes. She dusted the cobwebs off the old box and closed back the closet, locking it and placing the key back around her neck, dropping it between her big bosom.

Miss Millie sighed. She opened the old box revealing pictures, feathers, pieces of hair and rolled deteriorated papers she had placed into the box many years ago.

Gadé mizé mwen non! Miss Millie said to herself before she removed what seemed to be branches of *tree of life* in the bottom of the old box. She threw the plants into the bin at her feet and sucked her teeth as she removed the old pictures.

As she dusted the cobwebs off the items in her hand, one could see Janice standing at the corner of Miss Millie's house next to James. However, in the picture, James' head was cut off and what seemed to be sprinkled blood had dried over the old photos. As Miss Millie flipped through contents of the box, it revealed what some may have speculated but no one could reveal - Miss Millie had spent the last few years spiritually binding the Hopkins in *Obeah*.

It had long been speculated in the community that Miss Millie had ties with Obeah men and women on the island but no one wanted to list their eyewitness accounts to confirm those theories, as it would reveal the identity of the villagers who visited the Obeah men too!

Miss Millie had collected items from Janice and her family that she brought to Mother Sally and Captain Peter to cast spells on them: to cause rifts between the siblings, to break up Janice and James' marriage, to trap James in San Souci and to ultimately destroy to entire family union.

She remembered the moment Mother Sally had called her to tell her that she met James and the curse she placed on him seemed to work. The pair had spent a lot of nights in the shrine in Palmiste conjuring up spirits and spells to bind the Hopkins' family.

Miss Millie cursed the day James was able to leave; she knew it was Janice's trickle of hope along with her fervent prayers for James, when all seemed lost. Miss Millie didn't count on what James' love and devotion to his family or the support of family members and friends in prayer could do. They may have been bound by chains but love and faith set them free!

Glossary

aa: an expression denoting surprise

ah dey: I'm okay

allu: all of you

bavay (n): dried saliva around the mouth after getting out of bed

beh-bel-joe (adj.): a foolish or senseless person

bet me bottom dollar: bet one's last dollar; to be quite sure

big people business: conversations reserved for adults only

boot: to butt

bounce (v): colloquial term for knocking fists as a greeting

bring (brought) back news: gossip

bunjay!: A Grenadian French-creole expression denoting surprise, literally meaning *good Lord!*

bush bath: a spiritual cleansing done with special herbs by an Obeah man/woman

buss: to burst

cacadoh: a type of crayfish [see: *crayfish*]

cacajay (n): Grenadian French-creole term for dried eye mucus. *Caca* means faeces and *jay* is the French-creole variation of the French word *yeux*, which means eye

carriacou love: a phrase used to define the romance between two young lovers

chuhts/chuhts man/ah chuhts: an expression denoting annoyance

cocoa tea (n): hot chocolate made from grounded cocoa beans mixed with Grenadian spices

couldn't pull/can't pull: unable to agree with someone

cous': cousin

crayfish: a fresh water crustacean that resembles a lobster

cuff (v): to punch someone or something

cut-eye or bad-eye (adj.): to give someone a dirty look

cutlass (n): machete

cyah/cyan: cannot

dash: a mild version of the word *damn*, which is considered by some Grenadians as an obscenity

de beast with de long ears: description of an ass/ donkey; "*doh play de beast with the long ears*" literally means "don't be an ass"

donkey pee on me/you: to be entangled in bondage in the spiritual world through Obeah

donkey was in James cane (donkey in you cane): to be cheated on

dutty: dirty

eh-fwere!: A Grenadian French-creole expression denoting surprise

fadda: father

fares (n): money received for sexual favours; *to make fares* (v): the act of having sexual intercourse with someone for the sole purpose of financial gain

fass/fass'ness (adj.): to be extremely inquisitive

fe-oh-lay (v): to go out and party about

fore-day morning: very early in the morning

four-eyes: person who wears glasses; having an extra pair of eyes

gadé mizé mwen non: Grenadian French-creole phrase meaning "look at my trouble"

gyal/gyul: girl

hand of fig (n): a bunch of bananas

head hard: stubborn; hard-headed

hold me tongue: to remain silent

horn: colloquial term for cheating

hungry mout': to be greedy

jacket: when a man unknowingly raises a child that is not his (v); a product of infidelity (n) *jahpah* (adj.): unkempt

janet house: very small wooden houses built in Grenada after the destruction of hurricane Janet in September, 1955

ketch: catch

la diablesse (pronounced *la-jah-bless*): a beautiful woman who sold her soul to the devil. She wears a straw hat which covers her demonic face and a long, flowing, white dress which hides her one human foot and one cow foot.

licks/licking: beatings

lif' (or raise) you mudda nose: to make one's mother (family) proud

lougarou (pronounced *li-ga-roo*): the male version of a soucouyant [see: *soucouyant*]

mad blood: to go crazy

mama malade (pronounced *mama mah-lah-de*): the spirit of a woman who died in childbirth. She roams the street making the sound of a crying baby; anyone who looks out will have their souls taken by her.

mudda: mother

mullet (n): fresh water fish

mybone (n): Grenadian term for wasp

obeah: a form of witchcraft originally from Africa, that is practiced in the Caribbean

ol'-talkin': to chat informally

papa God: Father God

pumpkin vine: a very distant relative

real ha wayward ways: to be susceptible to straying

ridin' buddies: close friends

salt head/she head salt: phrase used in Grenada to describe when a person's hair is unable to grow past its short length

scrutch (n): colloquial term for one's crotch

shango baptist: a syncretic religion which combines the Spiritual Baptist religion (combination of traditional African beliefs and Christianity) and Shango, an orisha or god.

sorry (adj.): meaning pathetic, unwanted, stupid when used with another word. e.g., *sorry money, sorry excuse of ah man*

soucouyant (pronounced *sue-cou-yah*): an old woman who sheds her skin and shape-shifts. She lives alone in an old house by day and flies in a ball of fire by night.

study you head: keep on the right track; don't follow idle company

take you' nose outta people business if it en ha' no place dey: stop being nosy; don't inquire if it does not concern you

the biggest set ah balls: used to reference the bigger/ more mature of two men

thief: used in Grenada as an adjective(you too *thief*), noun (dat ol' *thief!*) and a verb (he *thief* de man money, wi!)

to close shop: to become celibate

to have de balls: to be very courageous

to play "hard-to-get": to not be easy enticed

to trap [crayfish]: the act of setting a specific trap to catch crayfishes

to trap [someone]: to bind someone through Obeah

tusty (adj.): used to describe someone who has a strong desire or wanting for the opposite sex

two cock cyah live in de same fowl coup: only one man can live under this roof (Mainly used by fathers when referencing their sons)

village ram (adj.): male known to engage sexually with several women in a community

wa de gyal (man, boy) say/ wa go?: informal Grenadian greeting meaning how are you?

washy-washy (adj.): a person who does not have much morals; anything goes

waste-ah-time-man (adj.): a man with little or no values

water nut (n): colloquial term for coconut

we is pig language: referring to the sound pigs make; the phrase used in Grenada literally means the statement is the view of one person and not the view of everyone else

wi: creole for the word *yes*, derived from the French word *oui*

wi, papa!: an expression denoting surprise, meaning "yes father"

Author's Note

Grenada, Carriacou and Petite Martinique is a tri-island state in the windward islands of the Caribbean. The island was seized and colonised by the French in 1600's, thus resulting in Grenada's various French-influenced village names and language. French-Creole, which is considered to be a mixture of two languages (African and French), is fluently spoken on the island by a small number of people.

French-Creole is not only spoken in Grenada; in fact, throughout the Caribbean, there are many variations of the language, such as: St. Lucia's *Kwéyòl*, St. Vincent's *Vincentian French-Creole*, Dominica's *Kwéyòl* and Haiti's *Kreyòl*. Many of the French-Creole words used in Grenada on a daily basis go unnoticed.

A few of the traditional ideologies and practices in Grenada, have originated from Africa, and were brought to the Caribbean through the slavery period. Many traditional practices such as saraca, big-drum nation dance, Shango and of course, its folklore, just to name a few, are aspects of Grenada's culture handed down by its African ancestors.

While the island's name and its dependencies have been used throughout this book, the holistic nature of *Chains that Bind* is fictitious. No names or places utilised represent any real person, place or entity.

It is the hope of the author that *Chains that Bind* encourages readers, especially young Grenadians, to explore Grenada's rich cultural history, its language and fascinating folklore.

Made in the USA
Columbia, SC
07 April 2019